Learning to love
Blue

SARADHA KOIRALA

A catalogue record for this book is available from the National Library of Australia

A catalogue record for this book is available from the National Library of New Zealand.

© Saradha Koirala 2021

ISBN 978-0-6451993-0-7 (paperback)
ISBN 978-0-6451993-1-4 (eBook)

First Published 2021

Cover and book design: Kellie Book Design
Editor: Anna Golden
Proofreader: Nichola Scurry

RECORD PRESS
29 Irvine Crescent
Brunswick
Victoria 3055
Australia

www.saradhakoirala.com

For Joni.

PART ONE

one

When Bob Dylan arrived in New York on 24 January 1961, it was the coldest winter in 28 years. Leonard Cohen and Joni Mitchell moved to New York a few years later, but I haven't read anything about their thoughts on the temperature. Well, they were both from Canada, where it snows all the time, anyway. Now, I'm not in New York and I'm not saying this is record-breaking weather, but my own musical migration to Melbourne will be historically marked by a sheen of sweat and 30 degree heat.

I put my bass down on the front step to shake off my cardigan and ring the bell, while the Uber driver unloads my luggage. It's not even nine in the morning yet, but I'm desperate to get into the shade.

Shaun opens the door and looks exactly as I'd imagined him, based on the slow drawl of his voice from our earlier phone call. His facial muscles are so relaxed he's gone beyond cool, to disinterested, nearing comatose. Black jeans, Chucks and a leather jacket over a band T-shirt I can't quite identify. I don't think this guy checks the weather forecast before he chooses an outfit. His hair is sculpted perfectly. He must have to get it cut weekly to maintain that kind of precision. I run my fingers through my own shaggy hair and smooth down my fringe.

Shaun's face twitches a 'Hey.'

'Hi, I'm Paige, Paige Bell from Mudwiggle – well,

from Wellington. I mean, I just called you from the airport, but I was using a new SIM card in my phone and it was such a mission getting here, perhaps you've forgotten!'

I blather on, overcompensating for his laconic silence. I feel exactly as I am – young, naïve, excited.

When I tried to sleep last night, it felt like I was hovering above the bed in a state of limbo, looking down on my restless body from the space where my Abbey Road poster used to hang; my room so bare and stripped of me.

Rose came down from uni to say goodbye and she and Linda got up this morning at the last minute to see me off, wrapped in their robes and rubbing their eyes. Dad was fussing about in the kitchen before I'd even emerged from my room, boiling the jug and trying to look as if it was morning. It was still pitch black when he drove me to the airport.

'I got you.' Shaun smiles almost imperceptibly and says, 'Welcome to Melbourne, yeah?' He lets me in.

The house is brick and concrete, much cooler inside than out. The rooms are so large it looks like the other housemates haven't moved all their stuff in yet. But there are homely touches too with the odd hanging plant and worn rugs and gig posters on the floor and walls.

The room that's available for me at the moment won't be available for long. It's a sublet and its rightful owner will be wanting it back in a few weeks. But it works for now, while I find somewhere more permanent.

Shaun helps me carry my stuff upstairs then leaves me to it. I sit on the bed. The empty room feels full of potential. My chest feels empty, but not in that familiar anxious, hyperventilating way. This is good. I feel high. Perhaps from the lack of sleep and barrage of newness. I look through my notebook – full of names, numbers, dates, addresses – I've been obsessed with planning since deciding to move countries. Now I'm finally here! I open my bass case and lay my precious instrument on the bed before heading back downstairs to introduce myself to my other housemates.

As the lovely early morning chill in the house is warmed away, the other occupants are stirring. They seem genuinely pleased to meet me.

'What are your plans for the day, Paige? Resting? Unpacking? Exploring?' Mel asks. She's tall and freckled with messy, mousey hair and the straightest eyebrows I've ever seen. Mel, Shaun and Lex are sitting on the couch in the lounge. I perch on the arm.

'Exploring sounds good. I also have the number of a guy to call about playing bass. Apparently he might be able to get me a job at ...' I look through my notebook for the name of the record store, '... Basement Records. Do you guys know it? Some guy called Jesse?'

'He plays in that surf-rock band, I think,' Mel says. 'Didn't you play drums with him, Lex?'

Do all drummers have monosyllabic names? I wonder if *surf-rock* is a genre I should know about. I write it in my notebook.

'Yeah, Jesse is amazing!' Lex nearly leaps off the couch and waves his skinny arms around as he tells me, 'You need to meet him! I don't know why he'd be looking for a bass player though – what happened to Carlos? Those two were a tight team.'

'Carlos started playing with Goldlust, didn't he? They're doing pretty well. Maybe he opted out of Jesse's band in favour of that gig?'

'Shaun, weren't you going to play bass with Goldlust?'

'They asked me to do a gig or two, but nothing serious,' Shaun doesn't look up from his phone. 'I'd play with them again if they asked though. Their shows are top-shelf.'

'We're supporting them at Old Bar this weekend.'

'We are?'

'I mean Nic Cage and the Bad Leads we, not Ghostwriters we.'

'Oh. Cool. We going?'

I've lost the thread of the conversation as my new housemates list the ins and outs of their tight-knit, multi-band scene, but I'm in awe. I love it. I am desperate to be part of this world.

Lex remembers my question. 'Oh, so Basement Records is really near here. You could walk over there and say hi to Jesse, easy.'

'Great. I'll totally do that. Thanks so much. I'm so glad to be here!' I'm beaming like an idiot, but I don't care. There'll be time to impress them later. Right now I'm happy being not even remotely cool.

*

Sydney Road helps me feel a little more normal and, although it's covered in hip stores and beautiful people getting coffees made with almond milk and riding bicycles through the terrifying traffic, there's a familiarity to it too. Op-shops, grocery stores, cafés selling caramel slice (just like cafés back home). It's busy, but people take the time to smile and let me pass.

People are people wherever you go. Bob Dylan said something like that. I'm aware that was 1960s New York with its Chelsea Hotel clichés. It's hard to tell if Dylan meant it in a good way or a bad way, but I like to think it's a good thing. These days it's Melbourne that's the music capital of the world. In fact, there are more live music venues per capita here than anywhere else, including London, LA, New York ... God, if I can't make it here, I can't make it anywhere.

Basement Records is bigger and grungier than

Foldback, the store in Wellington where I worked. It's playing louder music too and I feel momentarily daunted, but I am carrying a glowing reference from Will – my old boss, guitarist, friend and flag-waver – and so I head to the counter with my slightly crumpled CV.

The store isn't hiring, and it turns out Carlos *is* still playing bass with Jesse's band, Radtown. (I couldn't live with myself playing in a band with a name like that anyway.)

Jesse promises to keep my CV and an ear out for any other musical opportunities. 'You'll fall on your feet in no time, mate,' he says in the most Aussie accent I've heard yet.

I wander a little further until the day and the heat start to overwhelm me. I have one other number to call.

Spike knows I arrived today, but something's holding me back from calling. I don't want him to think I came here for him.

I retrace my steps to my room to do some more unpacking. I set my laptop up with some music playing and rip the duct tape off the cardboard box I brought from home. Thirty-five dollars for extra checked luggage, but I wasn't going to leave without my most precious possessions. I pull a few things out, but with nowhere to put anything, inevitably I abandon the idea of unpacking and pick up my bass. I'd better keep it unplugged until I've learned the house rules and routines a bit – I don't want to piss anyone off. I softly play along to some Nirvana that squeaks tinnily from my laptop speaker and do some cautious rocking out with the simplest of basslines.

The ripped-open box sits in the middle of the room and as I play I look at it, running through a mental inventory of its contents: cables, books and formative albums; Bob Dylan's memoir, *Chronicles: Volume One* (my leaving home bible); Joni Mitchell's *Blue* (with Mum's letter tucked into the liner notes); and *Wish You Were Here*. The title track of that album has been humming through my mind since I got on the plane. I've clearly been thinking about him.

Fuck it.

I grab my phone and send a text. *Hey Spike. I'm in Melbourne! I can't believe I made it! How's things?*

Then I throw my phone on the bed and vow not to look at it for at least twenty minutes.

*

In the evening, I walk to the supermarket with Mel. It wasn't worth paying even more excess baggage for things I could replace here, so I need everything – soap, shampoo, a towel, deodorant, tampons...

I keep checking my phone for a reply, but nothing yet.

'Do you know many people in Melbourne?' Mel asks.

'I've got numbers of a few friends of friends and there's a guy here I used to play in a band with.' I don't know why I just reduced Spike to that description. Things were so much more complicated than that. But I don't want to go into it all right now. What if he doesn't respond to my text?

'You'll meet people. There are so many musicians here and Kiwis and kids like you chasing the dream. Shaun said you're looking to get signed and play some of the big venues. That's not as easy, but you'll find your place.'

'Kids like me?' I laugh.

'Yeah. You're eighteen, right?'

Dylan was nineteen when he moved to New York City that cold January. He was signed to Columbia records by October. 'Why? How old are you?'

'I turned twenty-one last month.' She says it with such pride it sounds childish.

'I guess I'm used to being the youngest in my groups. I've been playing music with the big kids for years.'

'We are such fans of Mudwiggle, by the way.' Mel's

compliment disarms me. 'Shaun played us some tracks you recorded in the store. How come you guys never came over here on tour?'

A Mudwiggle tour was something I'd always hoped for. The band was already well-established when I joined and we performed every week, either at a bar in the city or a set-up in the corner of Foldback. Our practices became more like performances, too, with partners and flatmates sitting in to listen. We intuitively knew each other, musically. I'd been busy and fulfilled in my Mudwiggle days, but yeah, they were older. Will, the oldest, was in his mid-thirties, and he had the record store to run and a wife to consider. He couldn't leave the store and her to go off on a tour. Especially once she got pregnant. The guys in Mudwiggle were winding down their gigging days just as I was getting mine started. When Will broke the news to me that the band was breaking up, I had tried hard to hold it together and just be grateful for the time we'd had together. I almost managed it.

'We were a local band, really. The guys had stuff to take care of at home. It's cool to know we had a following over here though.'

I feel a brief wave of mourning. Then I reminded myself – things ending or people going away is not a rejection of me. Even so, it felt empowering to be the one who'd left this time.

The supermarket is smaller than I was expecting and all the items are in the wrong place. The shelves look different without my usual brands and I have trouble finding substitutes. I hadn't realised this would be something I'd have to adapt to.

Mel helps me find what I need. As I'm paying for it all, she asks, 'You want to come with us to the Goldlust gig tomorrow night? Lex is playing drums in the opening act.'

'My first Melbourne gig!' I squeal. 'I'm definitely in.'

'Good,' Mel replies without catching any of my excitement.

two

We walk up about a thousand stairs and finally reach a tiny venue, tucked into the back of a huge building that's leaking poppy synth tunes. Lex's band, Nic Cage and the Bad Leads, has already started. I knew we should have left earlier.

Mel and Shaun and I get drinks from the bar at the back then push our way politely to the front of a respectably-sized crowd. I've decided to just go with the flow at this point. I mean, I've been to plenty of gigs before, but this feels like a far cry from The Standing Room back home with its grumpy bar staff and decor that hadn't changed in a hundred years.

The rhythm section's pretty straightforward, but there's something impressive about the way Lex effortlessly plays drums. I've never seen anything like him. A lot of the tunes are anthemic, with dynamic choruses and emphatic lyrics, reminding me of the musically brilliant 80s. At other moments it sounds like nothing I've heard before.

The curtains close between acts – a nice touch – and when Goldlust starts they burst into their first song while the curtains are still opening. Mel tries to introduce me to a bunch of her friends, but Goldlust has our attention and it would take a natural disaster for them to lose it. We dance and I gaze at the musicians on stage with a kind of reverence, my drink sloshing rhythmically onto my hand as I move. I would give my left leg to rock that hard.

Hours later, we hurtle home through the streets on the tram, which is brightly lit and packed with people. I'm still in a state of wonder.

*

I can't identify the croaking noises. Frogs? Crickets, maybe? An owlish hooting sounds far away but won't let up. I can hear my housemates shuffling about, pipes creaking and gurgling, and an occasional shout from the street.

I thought I'd be exhausted, but my mind is buzzing and this bed is belabouring the point that it's not mine. I lie awake wondering where this bed came from, and why it remained in this room after everything else was removed. I wonder who else has lain here awake, perhaps contemplating the same things I am now. I miss my own bed and there's no fooling my body into thinking this is it. It faces the wrong way for one thing, and it feels old and tired.

At home, when Rose moved out to go to uni, I didn't hesitate before shifting her double bed into my room and sending my childish old single bed out. (Well, okay, there was some hesitation while I grappled with the logistics of dragging her surprisingly heavy mattress down the narrow hallway. It took ages and Linda had to rescue me when I thought I was going to have to sleep right there in the hallway forever.)

After four months in New York, Dylan got his break-out gig in April, opening for John Lee Hooker, but I don't know if I can wait that long. What a long, lonely road it must have been. When Mum gave me Joni Mitchell's *Blue*, I hadn't seen her in years and had no idea she liked folk music. She left me a note with the album, addressed to 'Little Green' (me, I presume), but when I listened to it, it felt too sentimental, too soppy. Did Mum really feel those things about love in the opening track? Just wanting to knit jerseys and wash someone's hair? I've tried to listen to *Blue* all the way through, but I usually skip to the happier songs – 'Carey', 'California', 'This Flight Tonight'.

The night crawls on and I wonder if it matters whether I'm well-rested or not. It's not like I have anything important to do in the morning. As the sky begins to lighten, I roll off the saggy bed and stumble downstairs. Glass of water, bathroom. Back to bed, read. I write a few things in my notebook, but I'm just passing the time.

*

People zoom past me as I wobble dangerously on my new bike. Wellington was too hilly and windy for biking, but apparently you never forget how to do it. Google Maps tells me my destination is a mere eight-minute ride away, but I suspect Google Maps hasn't seen me ride a bike. My new bike is second-hand, rickety and rust-coloured, but it was free and it'll get me around the city for nothing. I figure I'll get better at it with practice.

I'm finally going to visit Spike. I was surprised he lived so close – eight minutes. All the hours I spent over the last couple of months scanning maps of Melbourne were worth it. Shaun says all the best people live in the north. In fact, he warned me (I think jokingly) about wandering south of the river.

I have to stop and check my phone a couple of times to make sure I haven't missed a turn. The longer-than-predicted ride gives me more time to think. After Spike left for his sound engineering course in Auckland, and while Ed was recovering from his accident, everything changed. Starting Year 12 without Vox Pop, my band mates, and my sister had sucked. Even so, I'd managed to have a pretty good year. I still had Molly and Lily at school, and when Rose came back from uni in the holidays, she still slept in her old room (in my old single bed). When Ed was feeling better, he and I had road tripped up to Auckland to see Spike. We hung out in his grotty apartment in Kingsland and it had almost felt like old times, them talking music and me asking questions, eager to learn everything. We stayed two nights – me on the couch and Ed on the floor. We mucked around playing old Vox Pop tunes with Ed on a makeshift drum kit (upturned buckets featured heavily) and still sounded pretty good, even without Jay doing the vocals. The memory makes me laugh out loud.

When Spike came back to Wellington last summer, we caught up a couple of times, listening to records in his old bedroom at his folks' place. I'm pretty sure he was hoping I'd move to Melbourne too. The way he talked up the music scene, the bands and epic venues constantly looking to book acts, gigs every night. If I'm serious about playing, this is the place to be.

My relief at finding the right street is quickly replaced with excitement at the thought of seeing him again. I run through all the things I want to tell him about my first few days here – my housemates, the two gigs I've already seen, the things that remind me of home and the weird little differences I may never get used to – the supermarket, the lack of hills and sea, the Aussie phrases that make me laugh.

I'm chaining my bike to the fence outside, when Spike comes out to greet me with an enormous hug, nearly getting himself locked to the fence too as I throw my arms around him.

'Paige! It's so completely great you're here!'

He looks almost exactly like the Spike I know, but with floppier hair and better clothes. Well, similar clothes worn better – a checked shirt buttoned at the collar and cuffs, where in the past it would have been loose over a Led Zeppelin T-shirt. I am inordinately pleased to see his familiar dimpled face.

'It is, right?! And it's so good to see you! Hey, I can't believe how close we live.'

'All the best people live in the north,' he says.

'I've heard that.' I grin.

*

We go inside and his flat feels familiar with a similar authentic charm to the one Ed and I visited in Auckland. It's smaller than my new house and we squeeze past bikes and large speakers in the hallway to get to the lounge. He has a Queen record playing and I hope it's a sentimental nod to our past. Even if it isn't, I'm charmed that Spike's still a fan.

'So,' he sits down and looks at me. 'Tell me absolutely everything.'

I pause and look around for something to say. 'I love that you brought your records with you!' Spike's prized possessions are all in beer crates stacked against the wall of the lounge.

'Of course! I had my stuff shipped over pretty soon after I got here. How about you? Did you bring much?'

'Just my favourites really. I left a lot at home – maybe as insurance in case it all goes wrong and I have to crawl back there, tail between legs, you know ...' How easily my insomniac fears become a joke.

'Nah, you'll stick around, I reckon. This city is so you. What are you going to do first?'

'I need to find a band, man! Start gigging, get a job, make it big!'

'Not much then.' He laughs. 'Well, there are plenty of bands around. I'll keep an ear out and talk you up. Even if you just start with a few gigs as a stand-in while someone's away – they'll soon see how awesome you are.'

'Thanks.' I blush. Will I ever be good at taking compliments? 'I'm going to take my CV around some record stores, too, but I'll honestly do anything that will pay for rent and records.'

'Well, I know some good people. I reckon they might be able to help you out. This is so cool!'

I'm so glad I moved here.

I grin at him and he grins back. At that moment, a voice calls from the front door. 'Hi, Spike? Are you home?'

A girl appears, with a wave of dark hair and a cute vintage dress. 'Hey.' She looks a little surprised to see me and I make a quick judgement. She's just boldly entered Spike's house without knocking. Who does that?

'Hey, Lou. Uh, cool, you can meet Paige! Paige – Lou, Lou – Paige. Paige is an old friend from Wellington. She just moved here. What's up?'

'Hi,' I say. It sounds stand-offish and sulky.

Lou's handshake is limp, but she smiles broadly at Spike. 'Greg said you'd be home and that I could borrow his Korg for tonight's gig ...? I'm not ... interrupting?' Both are phrased as questions but seem like statements to me. I find myself staring at the bird tattoos on Lou's sandalled feet.

'Yeah, man. That's fine, then. Do you know where it is?' Spike's on his feet, eager to help her locate the keyboard. 'Won't be a sec,' he says to me.

I wait for ages as they rummage about in another room, unplugging things, shifting gear and talking about people and gigs I've never heard of. I start feeling a little anxious – I'm not part of this yet. Is this what jealousy feels like? The girl has style, confidence, presumably some level of musical ability and a damn gig tonight. And is something going on between her and Spike? I take a few deep breaths.

Spike helps Lou carry the Korg out to her car and I

wonder if that was my cue to leave. It feels awkward to hang around.

'I'm sorry about that,' Spike says, closing the door and returning to the living room. 'Lou's playing keys and singing at The Mary-Anne tonight. Greg's my housemate and has heaps of gear – we've been doing some recording, do you want to check out the studio? I'll show you around.'

I nod and get up.

Spike continues, 'Lou's great. You two would totally get on, I reckon. She's an amazing songwriter. If I wasn't working tonight, I'd totally be going to her gig. Hey, you should go ...?'

'She seems great,' I say. I'm definitely jealous.

Spike shows me around what must be thousands of dollars' worth of musical and recording equipment. I'm in awe and wonder how anyone could afford so much ... *stuff*. The tour ends at the front door and it feels like time to leave, though I would have loved to have stayed chatting.

'We live in the same city again!' I proclaim. It really has been a while.

'See you soon, Paige. Let me know if you need anything.' Spike hugs me goodbye.

I unchain the bike and pedal back the way I came.

three

'Heya. Paige, right?'

I'm surprised she remembers my name. I was convinced she hadn't taken it in when we met three days ago.

'Yeah. Hi, Lou.' Needless to say, I remember hers and I'm curious as to why she's at my front door.

'Spike told me you're living with Lex and Shaun, and I was like, I know them! So I thought I'd pop by and see you all.' She's in the house now, all charming smile and self-confidence.

So, Spike's intimidatingly cool friend Lou, who borrows his housemate's keyboard for purportedly amazing singer-songwriter gigs, thought she would 'pop by' and see my housemates because she heard I live here? Is that normal?

'Oh right. Um, Shaun's around somewhere, I think. Lex ... who knows.' It doesn't seem to matter what I say.

She's looking around the kitchen, browsing the bookshelves. 'You used to play with Spike in high school, right?'

'Ah, in a band, yeah, Vox Pop, we were ...'

'That's so cute!'

I cringe visibly. Who is this chick again?

'How was your gig the other night?' She doesn't seem to be going anywhere, so I change the subject, hoping a bit more conversation will clarify what I'm dealing with here. Don't get me wrong, I'm happy to make new friends, but I'm vibing something weird with Lou.

'The Grand gig?'

'I don't know ... The gig you borrowed Greg's keyboard to play?'

'Oh, The Mary-Anne! It was so lovely, and the crowd was really into it. That was one of the best shows I've played there, actually.' Her confidence is starting to look a little like narcissism.

'Good to hear. How do you know Spike?'

'Isn't he the best? He's so talented – and gorgeous.' She looks me in the eye as she says that and smiles a bright lipsticky smile.

My chest suddenly feels hollow, but not in the good hyperactive way I'd been feeling recently. I feel anxiety rising. It's hot in here. Lou's Australian accent – *eesen't he the beest?* – is grating on my nerves and I suddenly want her gone. 'Yeah, Spike's great ... did you play in a band together or something?' I don't know why I want to know how they met so badly. I could easily ask Spike, but my anxiety around this won't shut up. I can hear my own heartbeat.

'I was one of the first people he met when he moved here, actually. And then I heard him play and I was like, wow!'

I don't know what else to say to this person, so I go look for Shaun. I find him in his room with his headphones on. He takes them off when he sees me in the doorway.

'Hey, Shaun, Lou's downstairs.'

'Lou? Lou Key?'

'I don't know, man. I've only met her once and I don't know her, but she's here and she says she knows you guys. I don't know what she wants. To be honest, I can't handle her right now. She's kind of a lot ...'

'It's all good, yeah? She probably needs to borrow some gear or something.' Shaun comes downstairs with me.

I realise I'm on the verge of panic and have no idea why. 'Doesn't she have any of her own gear?'

I busy myself in the kitchen, feeling a bit embarrassed at my overreaction, but not enough to join Lou and Shaun in their weirdly one-sided conversation. Shaun looks so disinterested surely Lou's going to get the hint and leave. Eventually, she does.

'Bye, Paige! Might see you at the Ghostwriters gig. Maybe we could walk down together,' she calls as she's leaving, and I wonder if I've made a judgement error. What if she's the only person who ever reaches out to me and I blew it by freaking out at her forwardness? Maybe Spike told her I don't know anyone here, so she was being friendly. Maybe I'm a jerk.

'Was she oversharing again?' Shaun asks as he shuts the door behind Lou. 'She does that, yeah?'

'No, it wasn't that. I just got a weird vibe.' I don't want to entirely dismiss my feelings.

'She's a character all right. A good sort though, yeah? And you won't be able to avoid her, I'm afraid. She knows literally everyone.'

'Well, she certainly wants us to believe that,' I say.

*

Lex remains a rather mysterious member of our household, but I spend a bit of time with Mel and Shaun. Shaun's maudlin presence is growing on me, and I realise it's more of a style thing. Mel can be a bit serious, but they seem like kind people. With their encouragement, I've printed a stack of CVs and am going to take them around as many music stores as I can find. Record stores, gear stores, purveyors of classical music CDs – I'm not fussy. There's even a bookstore with a music section out the back that I'm going to try. So that's today's mission. I map out a route on my phone and start walking.

The first store on my list is called Mostly Music and has a CD rack out the front. It's total bargain basement stuff – $3 each or four for $10. I've never heard of most of the bands and there are a stack of generic compilations called *Relax* and *Chillout*. I peer through the door. 'Mostly' is a stretch. It's pretty dubious to call this a music store at all. I reckon you should have to have a certain quota, like more than 50% music, to use the term in your name. This should be called 'Mostly DVDs, T-shirts with quirky statements about gender stereotypes on them, and 80s computer game memorabilia'. It's an inauspicious start.

The next place looks completely amazing. It sits behind a padlocked wrought iron gate and I can't see in at all. I'm surprised I didn't walk straight past it. I bet it's the coolest place ever, the store of my dreams. It seems to be attached to a recording studio and I make a mental note to ask someone about it later. I briefly consider slipping my CV through the bars, but decide to wander on.

It's funny how things change in ways you don't expect them to when you move to a new place. I'm realising that in Wellington I spent a lot of time indoors – bedrooms, classrooms, band rooms ... It was an interior life that wasn't exactly introverted but was definitely introspective. Reflective. We talked a lot about things that were going on in our heads – thoughts, feelings, lyrics, music, creative inspiration. There was an excess of looking back too, especially in my last year of school. Me and my besties, Molly and Lily (god, I miss them!) would talk about old times together as if desperate to hold onto them. Premature nostalgia documented by our journals and careful selfies. It makes it easy to look back, but it makes it almost impossible to just enjoy those moments for what they were. Here, my life is more external, maybe just because I'm exploring a new city and walking or cycling everywhere. Here, it takes a bit longer to get from the bedroom to the band room and I find myself enjoying the outdoor journey. It opens up my thinking, as I wonder about people's lives and these streets that will one day be familiar to me, in a future I'm starting to imagine. Of course, as soon as I shut my bedroom door and try to sleep, my worries are there waiting to be mulled over.

I'm still not sleeping well.

I find the next store on my list. It's a narrow corridor of a shop and I feel conspicuous as I walk in. There's a vintage Roland keyboard out the front and stacks of old turntables. The walls are lined with second-hand records in varying conditions and categorised non-specifically: 'recommended', 'old school', '50s–60s' etc. It's not Foldback and Will would hate it here, but something about this place feels like home. I'm sweating a little as I approach the guy at the counter with a CV from my bag.

'You're from Wellington? Cool city,' he says, as he skims the page.

'Yeah. It is pretty cool, although I was itching to leave. Hometowns are always good to get out of, you know? You been there?'

'I went there on tour, what ten, probably ten years ago now. It was a good time.' He looks wistful. Of course, this guy was touring his band ten years ago. He has curly black hair, smells of a recent cigarette and I'm guessing he played in ... a classic Aussie metal band that formed in the 90s. Probably called The Flaming Roos or something like that.

I smile. 'Cool, yeah, there are some good venues there. I'm keen to get into the scene here though. I've already been to some epic gigs. Bands here are so ... brave. I'm totally inspired.'

I tell him the local bands I know of, and he gives me a list of others to check out. We talk for ages and I end up leaving the store with a small stack of records and a heightened sense of optimism. I don't even have a record player yet. Technically he didn't actually say there was any work going and, to be honest, it's probably not the most popular store in this part of town. Nevertheless, I must be grinning, because I feel my face physically drop as I bump into someone.

'Paige!' She's breathless, and she looks like she might have run quite some distance to bump into me.

'Lou! What the – ah … surprise.' I know so few people in this enormous city, why is it Lou I bump into? I check that my CVs are secure in my backpack and wonder if my hair's frizzed up in the heat.

'Where are you going?' She has a wide-brimmed hat on and an almost transparent dress. 'Shall we get a coffee?'

I feel grungy in my op-shop jeans and scuffed Vans. What is it with this girl?

'I'm on a job hunt, actually. I have a few more places to go to and—'

'Ooh, what kind of job are you after?'

I love my record store dream, but I don't want to share it with Lou. She'll think I'm a dork. 'I'm just taking my CV round a few local places. What are you doing?'

'I've just been having brunch with some girlfriends. We should catch up! Come on, I'll buy you a coffee. There's a great place near here.'

We walk to a café only slightly off my carefully planned route. There's a bit of a performance finding a table and deciding if we will be eating – *oh, let's just have a look at the menu anyway* – and I realise I'm completely not in the mood. But if I can't push myself out of my comfort zone in this small way, then what am I doing here?

Hanging out with Lou is actually pretty easy. She asks a few intrusive questions that I manage to evade and then she seems happy rambling on about all the people I should meet and the things I should know about living in Melbourne. I tell her I'm still looking for a band to join and she gets excessively excited about us playing together.

'I could use a bass player for some of my songs! I play basslines on the keyboard usually, but maybe we could start a girl band!'

I feel like pointing out both the borrowed nature of her keyboard and my objection to the patronising term 'girl band' but decide against it. Maybe she'd be fun to play music with. Spike said she's good and Shaun said she knows everyone.

'Okay, well, let me know. I have all my own practice gear and am itching to start playing again.'

Well then, shame on me for the dig about her gear. At least I'm keeping my options open. You never know where opportunities are going to come from.

I give her my number and thank her for the hot chocolate. I really have to keep going on my job hunt.

After leaving Lou, I find myself walking up and down the same stretch for ages looking for the next place on my list. It's an unlikely street for a record store. I followed the blip on my map into a dead-end suburban street with Aussie flags flying outside every house and car carcasses on the lawn, and now I have the sudden fear that this place exists only as a trap for young rockers, luring them towards this suburban backyard. Time to give up on finding Basement and Goldmine and Gutterblack. (Why do record stores have to have such forebodingly subterranean names anyway? It's creepy. Well, it's creepy when you're lost anyway.)

Next, I find Spin Records and it's record heaven.

There are two older guys – much older – chatting at the counter when I walk in, and the store is beautifully ordered. New and second-hand records are all in plastic covers and sorted according to genre. They each have a typed sticker on the front that gives a description of the album and its significance. It's like a library. There's the inevitable vast collection of Australian rock – all the AC/DC and Rose Tattoo you could wish for – but also an incredibly thorough collection of indie rock and garage. I'm torn between handing in my CV and just losing myself in the stacks. I'd start browsing, but I don't want to look too half-hearted about my interest in getting a job.

'Do you need any help?' one of the men interrupts his conversation to ask me.

'Yeah, hi. This is a beautiful store. I'm actually looking for work and was wondering if there are any shifts going here?' I offer my CV.

'I could take your CV, but to be honest, it would just end up in the pile.' He gestures behind the desk as if there's a teetering pile of CVs there about to crash down with one final addition.

'Right ...' What do I say to that? I'm still holding out my CV.

'People come in here all the time looking for work. I'm not trying to be harsh, it's just business really isn't good enough to take on more staff. Most people don't buy records.' Not being harsh would have been quietly taking my CV with a smile and putting it in 'the pile' without my knowledge.

'Okay. Well, thanks anyway.' I'm torn between wanting to continue browsing and just getting the hell out of there.

I've handed out exactly one CV on this mission and the more I think about it the less I want to work in that jumbled store with the guy reminiscing about the glory days of touring New Zealand. I'm determined not to feel defeated, but when the next place turns out to be permanently closed, I can't help it.

*

I keep my eyes peeled for record stores. I've been carrying my purchases for what feels like miles and I've strayed quite far from home. It's hotter than ever and I feel exhausted. I tune into a familiar sound outside a very cool looking café. They're playing the latest Stink Kitten single. At once, I feel both homesick and at home. The café is called Vinyl – it couldn't be more perfect.

'Hey!' I'm even greeted as if they know me.

'Hi!' I'm sweating again. 'Stink Kitten!' I point to the ceiling as if pointing to the sound. 'I know these guys!'

'Great track, right?' the guy at the counter says as he turns it up. The few punters in the café don't seem to notice. They're absorbed in their laptops and paperbacks. 'How do you know them?' he asks.

'From back home in Wellington. They won the Rockfest a few years ago and were kind of my heroes in high school. They moved over here, didn't they?'

'Yeah, they're mates of mine. Well, I know the bass player pretty well.'

I'm starting to expect that everyone knows everyone around here, even if they don't really.

'Are you after a coffee?'

'Oh, right. Umm. Not really. I'm actually after a job and a band and maybe a glass of water?' The heat must be making me chattier than usual.

'You're after a job? Can you make coffee?'

I don't even drink coffee and I've certainly never been interested in how it's made, but I feel the weight of the stack of CVs in my bag. I have to do something.

'I just need a job, man. If there's work going here, I'm keen as. There's a cool vibe.' I look around at the walls – gig posters from the 90s and a few portraits of the usual suspects, Jimi, Jim and Bob. There's a long shelf of records at the back and a stack of books.

'Well, if you have a CV I can give it to the manager. I trust it states your connection to the illustrious members of Stink Kitten.'

I laugh and hand him a copy.

'There's water over there. You look like you could use it.'

'You may have saved my life.'

four

'Paige! Paige, Paige, Paige! What are you doing exactly one week from tonight?' Shaun's holding his phone, pointing at me, yelling my name. I've never seen him so animated. It's terrifying.

'I have absolutely no idea! You tell me!' I was sitting on my bed reading when he burst in. I'm suddenly matching him in volume and urgency.

'Okay, so Goldlust asked me to play bass with them at Catfish, but I'm already committed and ...' he double checks his call is on mute, 'Frankly, they're getting a bit pissy about it, yeah? You free to play with them on Thursday?'

'Oh my god! Of course I'm free! Are you sure though? I haven't played with them before. They don't know me.'

'You'll be excellent.' Shaun's starting to reclaim his cool and become more recognisable. He puts a hand on his chest and sighs with relief.

'You don't actually know that.' I don't think he's ever heard me play, but I don't know why I'm arguing. This gig would be amazing. Goldlust!

'You used to play with Mudwiggle. I know more than you think, yeah?' Shaun gives me a wink then walks out of my room, talking authoritatively on his phone.

I can't believe it. I've got a gig. I throw my book on the bed, get up, grab my bass and start riffing out a bassline.

Catfish is still closed, but the doors are open, so I head inside. I've arrived ridiculously early for soundcheck. Well, actually I am exactly on time according to the message I got from the band, but no one else is here yet. And I mean *no one*. The band room is in the back of this old brick pub, on the way to toilets, but I've seen posters advertising tonight's gig all over town, so I'm hoping people will find us here. There's a separate bar and an elevated stage, which I dump my gear on. There are a few pieces of a drum kit, as most venues tend to have – bass drum, floor tom and a few cymbal stands – but I'm sure Tom, the Goldlust drummer, will move those in favour of the sweet vintage Ludwigs we've been practising with. He's a total pro. They all are. I feel the nervous excitement of throwing a party and being ready with the drinks and nibbles hours before the guests are due to arrive. I get my bass out and have a bit of a play.

Someone arrives to set up the sound desk. She calls out, 'Hey! Goldlust?' and I go down to introduce myself.

'Hi, I'm Paige. The rest of the band seem to be running late. I've sent a message and they're on their way.' I feel a bit embarrassed. Sound folk must get this all the time.

'All good. I'm Chloe. We can check the bass levels since you're here. Drums and vocals will have to wait for the others.'

I plug my bass into the amp on stage and play a few lines. I've practised with Goldlust a couple of times this week in the warehouse they use, but I'm not a hundred per cent sure of my parts without the rest of the band here. We fiddle with the levels for a bit, but again, without the band it's hard to know how loud I'll need to be. Chloe pops out, telling me to grab her from the front bar when the others turn up. I run through a few more lines on my own.

The rest of the band arrive all together and sure enough, the drummer has his entire kit with him. Although they set up quickly and get on with it, there's no explanation for why they're so late. Our soundcheck draws in a few punters and the start time of the gig is really close. There's another band on after us, so we play for about ten minutes, mumbling instructions to Chloe at the desk, then let the next band check their levels while we have a drink out the front. I think I thanked the band a thousand times for letting me play with them.

When we play to our live, packed, eager audience, I'm completely in the zone. Once the doors opened the venue filled quickly and when we emerged from the green room I was taken aback at how the place transformed from the empty room I'd been waiting in.

I'm tuned into the drummer and catching his eye regularly, almost oblivious to the lead section. My memory is pretty good – sometimes when you have to learn a part quickly it sticks better, like cramming for an exam knowing you can purge it from your brain as soon as it's pens-down time, but tonight I have to stay focused to keep it all in mind. Goldlust has a good following and I hear people getting excited when they recognise an opening riff, and they sing along. I'm not quite basking in the band's glory, but I could definitely get used to this. Their sound is similar to the garage rock I've been playing for the last few years, but there's a pop element too and they identify with the surf-rock scene, which seems to be big here. The crowd love them. (I mean, us.)

Afterwards, I'm sprawled on a couch in the green room feeling sweaty and wonderful, when a guy comes to sit next to me.

'Bunch up.'

There's plenty of room.

'That was an excellent performance.' He has floppy black Ryan Adams hair covering half his face. 'I love the way you play that – what is it? A P bass?'

'Yeah, vintage modified Fender Precision. Ace, right?' We're both looking over at where I've propped my bass in the corner. It seems to glow a little more sunburst, as if blushing at the compliment. 'I saved up for ages for it. I have a Warwick back home too, but I haven't played that for about a year.'

'*Beck hame*! Kiwi?'

'Ha! Yes. *Beck hame.*'

'Nice. How long have you been playing with Goldlust?'

'We've had a couple of practices, but this was my first gig with them. And actually my first Melbourne performance.' I'll never get tired of counting firsts.

'Well, you sounded like you've been playing together for ages. It was really tight. My band Agent Smith is up next. You coming out front to listen?' He holds my gaze until I answer.

'Yeah, of course!' I smile.

'Good! And afterwards we should probably go out and celebrate the success of your *furst Melbun gug iver*!' The accent mocking has worn thin already. He leaps up and goes out to join his band on stage. I head out front (enjoying that small spark of fame I always feel emerging from backstage) just as the crowd roars with enthusiasm and Agent Smith beats out its first notes.

Almost everyone I know is here. The feeling I had on my first day in town, as if everyone was connected through one band or another, has proven to be truer and truer. And I'm starting to feel like I'm part of it.

After the gig, we're all backstage drinking and hanging out. The guy from the green room is called Taylor. He's friends with my housemates. People gravitate towards him and his deep brown eyes. I feel buzzy and good as we talk about music and I tell him what it's like back home.

'I've always wanted to go to New Zealand – I've heard it's beautiful.'

'People keep saying that to me! I can't believe they don't just go. It's so close. Such a quick flight away.'

'I know! I guess there's a lot here to see too. I'm from Adelaide, so I usually go back there or explore Victoria when I leave town.'

'There's lots to see in New Zealand too, but we seem to have a stronger desire to get out and explore further afield. I figure home will always be there to go back to. I don't imagine much changing while I'm away.' It almost feels like I'm willing it, daring it to stay the same in my absence.

The staff are cleaning up the venue around us and we form a plan to move to a club in the city. We've packed up our gear and they'll lock it up here for us to collect tomorrow. I pick up my bag and check my phone. There's a message from Spike replying to my invite to the gig.

So sorry I couldn't come and hear you tonight – Goldlust! Awesome! Hope it goes/went well. I'm finishing up sound at Roxy now. Wanna hang?

I put it away unanswered and follow my new friends into the night.

five

'Hey, Dad.'

'Hi ... Paige ... Can you hear me okay? Is the camera thing on?' Dad's face is huge on my phone screen. He's peering into it as if he has to look across the Tasman to see me.

'I can see and hear you just fine. How's things?'

'Things are good! How are you? What's been going on in your life? I feel so out of touch.' He sounds a little panicked.

'You've been getting my messages though, eh?' I feel like I text Dad most days.

'Yes, yes I have. We miss you. What's the latest? Do you have a job yet? A band?'

'I played a gig last night! Just stepping in for a bass player who couldn't make it, but it was so amazing! And I've met so many great people ...' I decide not to go into any more detail with that one. 'But I have to move out of my room in a couple of weeks, so I'm on a serious job and house hunt.'

'That sounds so grown up! Why do you have to move? You don't like it there? Not your kind of people? You can always come home.'

'I know. I'm not coming home. Not yet. The room here was always a temporary thing. Hopefully I can find a house through some people I met here.' I'm determined not to mention Taylor, but the more I go on about 'the people' the more likely Dad will ask who they are.

'Have you seen Spike? Is he helping you out?' Dad's string of questions is exhausting, but I have to indulge him.

'Yeah, Spike's around. He's great. Same old Spike. He's busy though. He vaguely offered to help, but I guess I'll have to ask more specifically.'

'You were going to work on that, love, weren't you? Asking for help?' Linda has popped up in the background. I can see a snippet of her fluffy blonde hair and forehead behind Dad's gigantic face. The camera moves awkwardly to let her in.

'I know. It's hard to know what help to ask for sometimes though. Anyway, things are going well. I took my CV around some record stores and there's a café nearby that might be looking for staff.'

'A café? You could become one of those coffee experts.'

The problem with Facetime is that you have to suppress your eye rolls. 'I could. I love the idea of working in a music store, but it might not be very realistic. And I need to earn some money.'

'You need money?' Dad's big face again and another reminder that I can always come home.

'I'm okay for now.' I stop my mind from its persistent mental calculations. I know exactly how much money I have left. Not much. 'Depends on the kind of room I find, I guess. Some places are pretty expensive. But I'll be okay for a bit longer. Thanks, Dad.' I smile my best 'I'm okay' smile.

I would never admit to Dad how late I was up last night – and I certainly would never mention how bad it has made me feel. The call home has used the last of my energy. Lying down is my plan for the rest of today.

Last night we danced to bands in three different venues

and walked through the city in a large group, dominating spaces on the pavement, all talking and laughing at once. The streets were crowded, and I really felt part of something for the first time since arriving here. 'Celebrating my first Melbourne gig' is how Taylor described it. He stayed close all night and my heart raced when he sought me out on the dance floor or offered me his arm as we walked. At the end of the night, we caught the same tram – just the two of us – and he kissed me softly at my door. It felt practised, but not cliché; familiar, but utterly new. I've been smiling ever since.

Looking back through my phone I see that I never replied to Spike's message. I tap out a message now – apologising for the late reply and hoping he had a good night.

He sends one back straight away. *Argh! It would have been fun to go out last night! Just went home after work. What are you doing now? Come round?*

Simultaneously I get a message from Taylor. *Hey PB, had fun last night. What are you up to today?*

I'm going to have to think this through.

I head downstairs and find Mel at the kitchen table eating cereal and reading a book.

'Hey, Paige. How're you feeling after last night?'

'So tired!' I groan and slump into a chair.

'It was a fun night.' Mel states it as fact. It was fun. I knew it.

'So ... Taylor walked me home ...' I say, portentously.

'Taylor, eh? Did you guys ...?'

'No, we just kissed goodnight. It was all very PG. But he texted me just now. I think I need advice. What's his story?'

Mel closes her book and swivels in her chair. 'Taylor is charming. Completely. If he was kind to you and walked you home and was a gentleman about it, then that's genuine.'

I beam and start to respond, but she interrupts me.

'But – he does have a tendency to be charming and gentlemanly to several people at once. I'm pretty sure he's already seeing someone. Maybe multiple someones.'

Something in my chest caves in a little. She could have delivered that with a little more sensitivity.

'Some people don't mind that kind of thing, but personally, I wouldn't go there. He's gotten himself tangled up in some pretty ugly situations and you don't need to be making enemies of his girlfriends while you're wondering who he's with when he's not with you.' She pauses for the merest moment before going back to her book. Is this first-hand experience talking?

I type out two messages and send them off to their respective recipients. I don't feel like seeing anyone today.

*

I'm not used to having all this time to myself. It's like an extension of the summer holidays, but also kind of endless and friendless as well. I'm trying to do at least one useful thing around the house each day, but the house seems tidy enough most of the time. I need to hurry up and find a job. I'm churning through my savings just on day-to-day living.

I've spent this morning on my laptop scrolling through job listings for things I am either completely unqualified for or completely uninterested in or both. Some of these jobs don't even make sense to me – 'Experienced traffic controller' or 'Casual facilitator' or 'Brand ambassador'. I can play bass, write lyrics and sell records. That's really all I've got. Unless wasting ten hours a day on social media is an employable skill, I really don't have a lot going for me. Anyway, I just want to find a band. Gigging pays pretty well. I made $200 last week for that one gig with Goldlust. If I can get a regular spot somewhere, I'm sure I would start sleeping better.

Just as that thought forms and settles, my phone rings.

'Hi, Paige, it's Rob here. I'm the manager at Vinyl. You left a CV with one of our guys?'

'I did! Yes, I'm still looking for work.'

'Great. Can you come in today for a chat and a look around the café? We're a bit desperate.'

Gee, they must be if they've called me. I'm not even offended – the feeling is utterly mutual. 'I could be there in twenty minutes if that's good for you?' I'm already retrieving my shoes from under the bed and considering brushing my hair.

'Twenty's good, Paige. See you then.' Rob sounds like another old rocker living the rocker retirement dream.

*

I find my way back to Vinyl without too much of a circuitous route. It's about as busy as the last time I was here – people are reading and working quietly at the tables while some obscure indie band dominates the soundscape.

'We're a café, but we like people who know music and who care about vinyl. I see you've worked in record stores.' Rob leads me behind the counter to a small messy office and gestures for me to sit.

'Yeah. Just the one record store, actually. I was there part time for two years.' A bit of an exaggeration, but that's how these things work, right?

'I see that. Well, we're keen to train you up and give you some trial shifts if you're into it. Have you worked a coffee machine before?'

'No, I haven't.' I better not lie about that. I can hear the machine hissing and grinding from here.

'Okay. We'll train you when it's quiet. Until then we can have you taking orders, running meals, clearing tables and so on.' Rob hasn't smiled once, but it's pretty generous of him to take me on with no guarantee that I'm not crazy or incompetent.

'Thank you, that sounds amazing.'

'I know it doesn't look busy right now, but we're down a few staff and it's a competitive business. There are several other places people can – and will – go if they're not getting good service here.'

'It's a cool place. I really like the vibe. Thank you so much.'

'No problem.' He pushes himself out of his chair. 'I'll take you on a tour and then Caz will show you the ropes.'

A woman in her thirties with a red scarf tied through her hair and tattoos up her arms gives me a quick salute. She reminds me of Rosie the Riveter as she pulls the handles out of the machine and thumps the used coffee out.

*

My first shift leaves my legs aching and my mind buzzing. I hated not having a chance to talk about music and some of the punters didn't look me in the eye when I took their orders, but I text Dad as soon as it's over to tell him I'm earning again.

I decide to stop at Spike's place on my way home and let him know I've found a job. I still need a band and there's a part of me that would love to play with Spike again after all this time. We made good music together. Even Ed said that.

Spike answers the door with a sheepish smile, but lets me in.

'I should have called, but I just finished my first shift at my new job and I thought it was time for a catch up! You busy?'

'Your new job! Cool! Come in. I'm on the sound desk in a few hours, but I can be yours till then. So yeah, tell me all about work.' He flops onto the couch and I squeeze in next to him.

'Work was good. My feet are tired though. It was harder work than at Foldback, where I must have just talked about records all day, but it was fun learning something different. I'm just glad to be employed!' I kick my shoes off and pull my feet up onto the couch. 'It'll be a couple of weeks until I get paid, but then hopefully I can stop having stolen toast for dinner.'

'Stolen toast? What are you talking about?' Spike turns to face me, his arm stretched across the back of the couch. He's so close I can see the flecks in his eyes and hear the corners of his mouth lift into a smile.

'I mean ... borrowed. My housemate's bread. We name our food, presumably to stop others from stealing it and ... anyway ... forget I said that! I'm just looking forward to being paid.' Something about the way Spike's smiling at me makes me want to stop talking immediately. The comfortable silence grows a little awkward as I feel his breath on my face.

'Are you blushing?'

'No.' I give his shoulder a gentle nudge and leave my hand there. He takes my other hand and holds it up as if measuring my fingers against his.

Then the front door opens and closes with a clunk.

Spike leaps to his feet. 'That might be Lou. You guys have met.' He states this as if daring me to argue.

Yeah, we've met. Ubiquitous Lou.

Spike greets her in the hallway and tells her I'm here.

'Paige!' She strolls in and settles on the couch beside me. 'What are you up to?'

I shove my shoes back on. What does Lou do for money? Everyone else seems so busy and she's just hanging out everywhere I want to be.

'Hey, Lou.' Of course, I'll still be nice. I can't help it. 'I just had my first shift at Vinyl. I got a job at last! Remember? I was on the hunt last time I saw you.'

'Oh yeah, you were really struggling.' Does Lou patronise everyone, or just me? 'Are you making coffee, then? Spike said you used to work in a record store.'

Spike's disappeared. Is he in the kitchen?

'Yeah, well, I was getting a bit desperate. How do people live here? It's so expensive!' I look at Lou as if she might take that cue to tell me where she works. 'But I love Melbourne,' I go on. 'I'm happy just to earn enough money to stay.' I lean in the doorway feeling like I should leave, but not wanting to.

'Do you need help finding a band or meeting people or anything?' Spike returns holding a pedal and hands it to Lou. She doesn't even play guitar. Weird. 'I feel like I've hardly seen you.'

'Well, I do have to move out of my room soon and yeah, I still need to find a band.'

'Oh my god, this is perfect! I'm looking for a new housemate!' Lou squeals and leaps a little out of her seat.

Spike winces, and I force a smile.

six

I'm reading a long email from my sister while Led Zeppelin plays through my tinny speaker. I really need to get myself a record player and stop listening to Spotify. Maybe after a few more shifts at Vinyl – and once I've found a permanent abode – I'll have a look for one. I should probably buy some grown-up stuff too. Pillows and towels and cleaning supplies. Is that what grown-ups do?

Rose writes long letters and rarely chats online. (She's a bit old fashioned in that way.) I enjoy reading about uni and study and about some of the friends I met when I last visited her. But there's other stuff in this email. Mum stuff. Rose is good at keeping in touch with Mum, but I still have unread emails and missed calls from her. I'm not ready to treat Mum like she's family again.

I stop reading and flick over to scroll through my friends' Instagram feeds. Molly and Lily's latest escapade at some uni orientation gig in Christchurch. They're dressed up and look so much older and drunker than they were when we used to hang out. It seems a lifetime ago that we cooked dinners together and walked to school, playing cards and staying up chatting. I miss those days sometimes. Did I make the most of them? I feel less and less like a kid the longer I'm here, worrying about housemates and rent and motivation. I scroll through pictures of Ed with his music school band at a recent gig, although Ed's obscured in most of the shots. My amazing friend Sam, who moved north after high school, hasn't posted anything in a while. I can't remember the last time I heard from him. I hope he's found his place somewhere. Jay is ranting about some new band he loves ... Maybe nothing changes after all.

Scrolling a bit more, I find I am suddenly utterly homesick and lonely. I flick to my own Insta and look for the photo of Rose, Mum and me taken on Mum's first visit after leaving so many years ago. I scan our faces for similarities, Mum's crinkly-eyed smile looks a bit sad, but I reckon Mum looks like Rose. Rose reckons she looks like me. My eyes have clouded with tears and the three of us blur together, all with dark hair and brave smiles. 'Black Dog' is playing on my laptop and it's such a great song that I let the sorrow well up even though I have no idea what to do with it.

When Mum told us about her diagnosis last year, I had so many people checking on me and caring for me, maybe I took it a bit for granted. Rose, Dad, Linda, all my friends, the counsellor I saw twice before deciding it was too hard to talk about ... Now I've pushed all those people away and for what? A few shifts at a café, some awkward new friendships and the hope of playing on a stage someday. Perhaps Mum and I are the same after all.

Since I'm already feeling bad, I decide to finish reading Rose's email. Sure enough, the Mum news sucks.

My phone buzzes with a call.

Lou.

I'm just about to reject it when I remember my loneliness and soon-to-be homelessness, so I suck it up and answer. 'Lou. Hi.' I hear how flat my voice sounds.

'Paige. How are you, love?' I stall at the endearment. She continues, 'I have a gig in a couple of weeks and thought you might like to play bass for it? We would need you at some rehearsals – Wednesday and Thursday nights. Sound okay?'

I know I'm not in any position to turn her down. Especially the chance to play on stage again. 'I'd love to. Where's rehearsal?' Maybe I could become a session musician. Maybe that's my destiny. (I'd prefer to have a rock-solid place in the rhythm section of an amazing Melbourne garage band, get a regular gig at Cherry Bar, be picked up by a talent scout and signed to Milk Records, but for now this will do.)

'I'll text you the details. I have a few solo pieces and a few I'd like to do with a full band. This is going to be fun!'

'Yeah, it will. Thanks.'

'Also, have you thought any more about moving in here? You'd have to meet my other housemate Izzy and make sure we can all get along, but the room's available if you want to check it out.'

This might be a step too far. I feel anxiety creeping into my chest again. 'I haven't really had a chance to think about it. But maybe I could come and have a look on Wednesday? Before or after rehearsal?'

'Sure, I'll text you later. Ciao.' She snaps the conversation to a close. I can't shake my initial judgement of Lou, but she is trying to include me at a time when I'm feeling left out. I should be grateful she's making an effort.

*

'... I guess it just infuriates me that people go to such lengths to hurt living breathing creatures, so they can enjoy a fleeting moment satiating their – what? – bacon craving? It's disgusting. And research is proving it's also deadly.'

'Oh god, you're so right. Bacon is the worst. I mean, the best and the worst.'

'It is. I mean, I love the taste of bacon, but it just comes at such a cost. You know?'

Against Mel's advice, I'm meeting Taylor for coffee. I'm perfectly capable of doing this without any complications, right? I realise how unusual it is for me to go to so much effort for some company. At home I could call Lily over at the drop of a hat and not have to rehearse the conversation three times before phoning, or write lengthy disclaimers about how coffee is not a symbol of impending romantic entanglement. I didn't need to give a reason why I might suddenly want her company. I miss Lily.

Taylor's still explaining why we should all be vegans and I'm starting to feel guilty about the burger I was planning to eat later.

'It's so ingrained in our society, it's hard to shift people's mindsets. I mean, my family, for example, can't understand why I won't just eat pork dumplings and congee with them, but even just one person deciding to stop eating animals can make such a difference.'

'Okay, sign me up. You sound like the Vegan Society of Australia is paying you commission for recruitments. I'm in.'

'Ha. Sorry. It's my passion! That and music. And ... well, shoes actually. I really love well-made shoes.' I peek under the table and, sure enough, Taylor has amazing shoes. Two-toned high-top sneakers in tan and navy.

'They're vegan, I swear!' he says in response to my awed expression. Vegan shoes. I am certainly not in Kansas anymore.

It's time to start my shift at Vinyl so we make moves to go our separate ways.

'Come round to mine after, if you like. We can listen to that album I was chewing your ear off about.' Taylor looks me in the eye as he talks.

'Thanks,' I say. 'Can I see how I'm feeling at the end of my shift? This hospo work is taking it out of me a bit.'

'Of course. Text me.' He gives me a squeeze on the shoulder before heading off.

*

My shift ends with the most exhausting and demoralising task of all – mopping the floor. It's the last thing I feel like doing after six hours of running coffees and taking orders, but I want to finish in time to hang out with Taylor again, rather than heading back to the silence of my room.

Taylor's place is a tram ride away and I'm grateful to sit down for a bit. There are several incredibly well-dressed people standing, holding the rails, engrossed in their phones; a few kids in uniform who must have stayed late at school carrying tennis rackets and violin cases; a couple of elderly people with bags by their soft-soled shoes that they guard with menacing glares. There's a smell too – hot people crammed in a tin. It becomes increasingly unpleasant as I watch for a familiar landmark to identify the right stop. It's still hot out and I'm starting to accept that no matter where I'm going, however near or far and however I'm getting there, I will inevitably arrive covered in a sheen of sweat.

Taylor lets me in. There are lots of people milling about – making food, playing guitar, reading in the lounge.

'Still hot out? You look like you could use a drink.' He smiles at me. 'I mean, you look great, but I bet you could use a drink, huh?'

Such charm. What am I doing here?

'Umm, yeah, sure. The heat and the tram and the mopping of café floors ... I'm tired!' I put the back of my hand to my brow, melodramatically.

'Yes! Sit. I will bring you things. Meet ... everyone.' He

gestures towards a chair in the lounge and waves his arms at everyone. 'Hang out. You're safe now.'

Taylor brings me a drink and then takes a guitar off someone mid-strum. He starts playing out a familiar riff – The Strokes' 'Someday' and soon we're all singing it together, tapping out accompanying beats. I wonder if it's like this here every night. I'm in my element as the guitar is passed around and we each have a turn. I only know a few chords and a couple of Bob Dylan tunes, but Taylor talks me up as a bass player and I reiterate my enthusiasm for finding a band. Maybe one of these people will need a bass player. This definitely seems like the kind of crowd I should be in.

The thing about seizing opportunities when they're presented is that it's really difficult to know when to stop seizing. One drink becomes several, a casual hang becomes ordering takeaways with a bunch of people you've just met, listening to an album together becomes, well ... it can become very intimate. I'm sitting on the floor leaning back against the chair Taylor's sitting in and I have no idea what time it is. We're listening to some completely amazing melodic synth rising and falling on a seemingly endless track. The guitar has been passed somewhere far away, but I can still hear some gentle fingerpicking. My eyes are closed and Taylor's rubbing my shoulders in a way that's giving me goosebumps. I am properly relaxed. If someone poured me into that lumpy old bed of mine that I swear I've spent more time awake in than asleep, I think I would sink right in and never wake up.

As it happens, I wake up fully clothed on the couch in the lamp-lit empty lounge. I'm embarrassed to think people must have gone home and to bed around my slumbering (possibly drooling and snoring) body. I don't waste any time gathering my things and leaving quietly through the front door. I just hope I can find the tram stop.

Whenever I drink these days, I tend to wake with a feeling of dread – what cringe-worthy thing did I do or say? Who did I upset? Who did I flirt with?

I check my phone – nothing new, except a warning that my battery is low – and head down the street. I'm utterly disoriented but determined to find my way to the tram. I try to recognise the street names and decide to conserve my phone's battery by not using Google Maps. The night is still warm and I wonder if I'm in the wrong place at the wrong time of year. No need to shelter from the storm tonight. Am I chasing a dream in the wrong hemisphere? In the wrong decade?

Taylor's street is well-lit, but when I come to the end of it, I see that the laneways and alleys that are so quirky and charming by day, look like dark potential murder spots by night. I can hear voices further on and guess that must be the direction of the main street. My shoes clomp and echo on the cobbled path. I'm only just awake – I probably should have stayed on the couch. How can I talk to Taylor again after sneaking out of his house in the middle of the night like a fugitive?

It's too late to go back now. Something clatters down one of the alleys. I straighten and stride more purposefully. Sure enough, I'm approaching the main street. I wish I'd paid more attention when I arrived in the still-light evening, but I was busy on my phone, thinking about Taylor, trying to shake my exhaustion from work. Which reminds me – crap! – I have to be back at Vinyl for the early shift in the morning.

I can see the tram stop in the distance and I'm grateful I'm wearing my sensible work shoes and not some silly dress-up shoes that I might have been tempted to change into if I'd had the time. Function over form forever. A car screeches past, sounding like the driver left the handbrake on or the muffler's fallen off. It's straddling both lanes. I try to distract my thoughts from the terror of walking strange city streets alone in the dark. I'm not going to tell myself how foolish this is – there'll be time for that later when I'm safely tucked into my lumpy bed for a few hours before dawn.

I cautiously cross to the tram stop and check the timetable. I feel very exposed and there could be a long wait. It takes me a while to make sense of the list of tram times. It's a weeknight after midnight. There are no trams until morning. I can wait five hours here or have a very long walk home.

After sending three texts without a response, I bite the bullet and call Spike. I hate being that friend who wakes you in the night because they've got themselves into a stupid situation, but here I am walking in what I hope is the vague direction of my house in the middle of the night with my battery on red and my heart pounding at every noise that passes.

Spike doesn't answer.

I'm so used to cycling or getting public transport now that I had forgotten how slow walking is. A twenty-minute tram ride from work to Taylor's takes over an hour on foot. And that would only get me as far as Vinyl.

I check my phone again for signs of life.

It's nearly 2.30am. I need to get home, charge my phone, try to sleep, and be up again at 6am for a day of roaring coffee machines and customers with high expectations. At least the early shift means I won't have to mop the damn floor.

With its last gasp of battery power, my phone bleeps off. Relatable.

I give in to the walk and pick up the pace. If I follow the tram line back to work, I know how to get home from there, no trouble. I try to figure out what my impetus was for leaving that softly-lit couch scene back at Taylor's. Embarrassment? Did I feel unwelcome? Why didn't I just go back to sleep and catch the tram to work in the morning like a civilised normal person? I've slept on couches before. I could have handled it.

I start humming 'Don't Think Twice, It's All Right' to myself, walking along my own road, taking comfort in the 'it's all right' part. It's also the best song about moving on ever written.

A large group rounds the corner and I freeze. They're singing and having a great time, taking over the footpath and waving their bottles in the air. I take a deep breath and stand up straighter. It's all right, I tell myself again – I'm going to get home. They get louder as they approach, but also louder as they spot me, a potential audience for their clamorous show. One of the guys stares straight at me as he wails some lyric that's apparently speaking to him right now. I give my most unimpressed-but-not-trying-to-pick-a-fight look.

'I know you!' he yells at me.

I shake my head and deadpan a response, 'No, dude. You don't.'

But he stops walking and points at me, blocking my path, his other hand holding a Coopers bottle aloft.

I focus on trying to control my breathing.

'Guys, I know her!' His group has charged on ahead, leaving him behind. Every part of his face is exaggerated and he spits as he talks. He's in a good mood at least, but god, I need him to get away from me.

'Can you let me past now?' I'm still deadpan, but my heart is racing.

Someone calls back, 'Leave her alone! Hurry up, Simon.'

'Wait! I know her!' he replies. He doesn't look familiar, but then he probably doesn't usually look like this. His eyes are round and wide, his pupils so big his eyes look black. His face and hair glisten with sweat. I can smell his boozy breath. 'I know you!' he shouts again. 'I met you! You're Adam's friend!' I have no idea who Adam is. For a brief moment, I thought maybe I *had* met this guy or he'd seen me perform with Goldlust. But now he's lost me, and I don't want this guy shouting at me anymore.

I look him in the eye and speak slowly, 'Let me past. You're scaring me. You don't know me and even if you did, it doesn't give you the right to shout at me in the street. Let me past now.'

He backs away, raising both hands. Some beer splashes out of his bottle and he stoops slightly in a clumsy kind of bow. 'Sorry. I didn't mean to scare you. We're cool, right? You can pass.' He staggers out of my way.

One of his friends comes over. 'Dude, what are you doing?' He laughs, leading him away and calling back to me, 'I'm sorry. Sorry sorry sorry.'

I feel like I'm part of some binge drinking culture footage commenting on why youth are ruining everything for everyone. I'm shaking, but I stride on, proud that I stood up for myself. My instinct is to scurry down a back street so I won't be seen, but I know that's idiotic and I should stick to the main drag where trouble can be lit. My imagination is still running wild.

With my phone dead, I have no idea what time it is and no way to contact anyone. It's unlike me to let my battery run down. I can't even listen to music to distract myself from the eerie silence, so I start singing softly.

I'm exhausted, but things are starting to look familiar. I follow my nose down a side street and sure enough, I'm back in my neighbourhood. A wave of relief washes over me. I can't wait to crawl into my bed. Tomorrow is going to be rough, but all I can think is 'bed good'.

I head past the council flats, the park, the string of shops with their grated and graffitied corrugated doors. They hardly look like shops at all at this time of night.

At my house, I let myself in. Downstairs is full of hazards, but I don't care much when I bash my shin on a dining chair or when I step on something slimy. I head up to my room almost hysterical with relief, laughing to myself at the idiocy of it all. I plug in my phone and lie staring at the ceiling until my heart rate slows.

I sleep for what feels like mere moments before my alarm demands I be conscious again.

When I check my phone, I find a litany of messages from a worried Spike.

seven

Moving day. I'm leaving my first ever home away from home and luckily I don't have much to pack. I shove my few belongings back into my suitcase and put the overflow in a couple of boxes. I feel a brief sentimental pang as I pat the lumpy bed goodbye and carry my stuff downstairs.

Shaun gives me a lift to Lou's place and there it is – I've moved in with one of the only people I know here. Lou is now my friend, housemate ... and the object of my wary suspicion. Not to mention my potential band mate. God, if we worked together too there would be no escaping her.

I push that ungrateful claustrophobic thought away and carry my suitcase into my new room.

'You're welcome back round anytime, yeah?' says Shaun, as he dumps my boxes unceremoniously on the floor.

'Thanks, man. And thanks heaps for getting me set up. I really appreciate it.'

'My pleasure, Paige. Ace having a bass-playing buddy in the house. See you soon, yeah?' He's hard to get the measure of, but I take the sentiment for what it's worth. I'll miss him and his surly offhand company.

'Yeah, course. Catch you round the traps, as they say here.'

'They do say that! We'll make a local of you soon

enough, yeah?' Shaun grins and gives me a quick hug before leaving me to it.

Another room, another borrowed bed.

*

'You should have seen it, Paige! Molly was hilarious. You would have been so proud. He had no idea.'

'I wish I had seen it! It sounds amazing, Lil.'

'I can't believe how opinionated some of the guys here are. They start these arguments based on no real information and then don't have a leg to stand on when you challenge them. It's infuriating, but also totally fun. Half the time they're arguing that we don't even need feminism, which completely proves why we do!' The Lily on my screen is so animated, I can hardly believe it's just a little pixelated version of her in there, just image and voice.

'Anyway. What super exciting things have you been up to? Are you loving it? Is it amazing? You're so brave, following in the footsteps of your musical idols!'

I won't tell Lily about my bouts of loneliness and anxiety. Even though I know that telling her is exactly the kind of thing that would help me feel less lonely, I don't want her to worry about me. I want her to keep thinking I'm brave.

'It's pretty fun, yeah. I've been working at this café called Vinyl – it's totally rock and roll and Caz who I work with told me about all kinds of amazing underground scenes. She's an artist and makes these kinds of disturbing, beautiful sculptures. I think they're comments on the state of the welfare system here or something. I don't really get it. I'll send you a link to her Insta. Umm, I'm in a band. We haven't had any practices yet – we were supposed to, but they got cancelled – it's with another chick, who's also my new housemate. She's a keyboard player. I'm so used to being the only female in the band, it will be good to play with another girl.'

'Cool! Is Spike in the band too? Are you two together yet?' For all Lily's strident feminism, I knew she would ask.

'We're not together and he's not in the band. He's super busy, but we've hung out a few times. I don't know. I really wanted to get established a bit here on my own first, you know? To prove I can do it by myself. I mean, I don't want him to think I moved here for him. And what if I mess it up?'

'Then you come home. You'd be sad and it would suck, but we'd be here for you. Anyway, he's hardly going to reject you! Spike's loved you for years. And what if you wait so long he thinks you're not interested?'

'I don't know. Maybe.' I still can't see myself making the first move. Spike and I have a long history of awkward friendship. Who am I to ruin that?

'You know I'm right,' Lily winks at me. 'I should get to class. Are you getting out of bed today?'

'Ugh, I suppose I'd better. I miss you! Come visit me! I have a proper place to live now – there's just three of us living here. You could sleep on the couch or the floor of my room or we could just stay up all night. I keep seeing places I want to show you and things you'd find funny or cute or charming.'

'We will! Molly and me, we'll both come. Promise. We'll make a plan tonight. We miss you heaps.'

Despite myself, I feel my eyes filling with tears. I smile through them and wish I could reach into my screen and hug my best friend. She's tearing up too and we end our catch up with sobbing, laughing, sloppy goodbyes.

*

'I just gave you my order. Like, moments ago?' This

indignant customer is gaslighting me. Or I'm losing the plot. I'm sure this is the first time I've come to her table, and now she's making me question everything I know to be true. I am underslept, sure, but I'm not crazy.

'You've already ordered?' I ask, oh so politely.

'Two minutes ago. With you!' Her heavily made-up eyes widen. She looks like she's going to burst with horror at what she falsely assumes is my terrible memory.

Vinyl is humming steadily with the Saturday afternoon crowd, but we're not rushed off our feet. The same principle applies here as it did at Foldback – just deal with the customer in front of you. If you do it well, it shouldn't matter how long the queue is.

'Perhaps Caz took your order?' I gesture towards Caz as she strides past. We look nothing alike.

'Whatever.' The woman loses interest, going back to her giant pink phone with her giant pink finger-nailed hands. I bite my tongue.

When I tell Caz at the coffee machine, she rolls her eyes. 'While I'm flattered to be mistaken for an eighteen-year-old, all us hipsters look the same to people like her.' I'm shocked at the easy way she labels us as belonging to the same group. And quietly a little pleased.

'I'm a hipster?' I laugh.

'Oh, come on! A chick bass player who loves vinyl? Your Levi's and vintage band shirts? Your fringe!' Caz gives my thick fringe a quick flick. 'You're a hipster. Let me guess what's in your canvas backpack over there. A notebook? Poetry? Something you bought at the organic store?' She grins at me. 'AND you're resisting the label. That's a true hipster if ever I saw one. It's a beautiful thing,' she concludes, before switching on the grinder and drowning out any protest from me.

I'm still grinning when a familiar face appears at the

door. 'Spike! Hi. You here for lunch?'

'Hey, Paige. No, I'm just here to say hi, grab a takeaway coffee and invite you out tonight. Come to Roxy, I'm doing sound for this cool band I think you'll like. They're launching a single – I'll send you the link.' He gets his phone out.

'I'm keen. Was just thinking you and I should hang out more.'

'Absolutely, we should! I will be working tonight, but we can hang out between sets. It should be quite the party. Tell Lou.' He must notice my face twitch at that. 'I mean – you guys live together now, yeah? If you want her to come, let her know. It'll be fun.'

'Yeah, sure.' I snap myself out of a brief moment of jealousy. 'It sounds great. What coffee are you after?'

'Black coffee, large – the first of many. It's going to be a long day.' It's after midday, but I suspect the waking hours of a sound guy are kept differently from the rest of us. I put the order through but don't have time to chat much more. I give him a quick hug before carrying two plates of smashed avo on toast to a table outside.

I forgot to ask Spike if there would be a door charge. If I have to pay to get in, I just won't buy a drink.

Living with Lou has actually turned out okay. In fact, most of my interactions with Lou have been fine, so I'm starting to think the problem is me. The way we met at Spike's place, the way she's always around – it sounds like a me-problem.

At home, I tell her about the Roxy gig, but it turns out she was planning to go anyway.

'Spike's on sound? That's perfect! I'm so glad you're going too. Should we have drinks here first? I could get the girls round – we were going to meet there, but why not make a night of it?' Her enthusiasm is contagious.

'Okay! Let's do it! I'll see if Mel and Shaun at the old house are keen too.' I haven't been in touch with them since I moved out. And – even more bad form – I haven't messaged Taylor since my midnight walk of shame. He hasn't tried to reach me either though. How did I maintain friendships in the past? This feels like hard work.

'Yay! What should we wear? What should we drink?' Lou does a little skip and I'm briefly reminded of Lily and me getting ready to go out. If I put my mind to it, I can channel that girly sense of excitement for clothes and hairstyles again, I'm sure.

Mel arrives when we're ready to leave. Until then, it's just been Lou and me getting ready and hanging out for the last few hours. I wonder who 'the girls' were that she mentioned earlier and realise that I know very little about her circle of friends. Apart from our aloof housemate and Spike, I've never seen her with anyone else. I feel a twinge of pity – that horrible judgemental feeling disguised as sympathy and concern. Who am I to talk? I only have her and Spike, myself.

Mel and Lou don't seem to get on too well. I find myself in the middle as we walk to the venue, trying to engage them both in conversation. I remember what Shaun said about Lou having a tendency to 'overshare' – that doesn't seem like something Mel would warm to.

When we arrive, the place is packed. A darkened room is filled with the hippest people in Melbourne. They nod along to the music, making eye contact and stepping back respectfully as we enter. It's lovely – a rock community with a shared love of well-crafted music performed on top-notch gear. The cover charge will totally be worth it, I tell myself, and do a quick mental calculation of how soon I can earn it back.

Spike's in work mode, tweaking mics and talking to

the performers, but he gives us a grin and a nod when he sees us.

Mel finds some friends and introduces Lou and me before shifting further away from us and closer to them. Lou's 'girls' don't seem to be here after all. I feel that twinge again and decide to be the best company I can be for her tonight. You never really know a person.

Spike was right about the band. This is totally the kind of music I love. Technically impressive and musically original, harking back to the early days of rock when lyrics and melody mattered. The singers can actually sing and the bass player is working as hard as the lead guitarist. I get so absorbed I don't notice Lou disappear. But something doesn't feel right. I push through the crowd and linger near the sound desk until there's a break in the set and Spike has a minute.

'Hey! Do you love it? I told you you'd love these guys. Check out the dude's Maton – such a beautiful guitar. So Melbourne.'

'And the guy with the Strat! Yeah man, I totally love it!' I'm shouting, even though the music's stopped. I take a slow breath. 'Have you seen Lou? I can't find her anywhere. D'you think she might have taken off?'

'Nah, she'll be here somewhere. She probably just saw someone she knew.' Apparently, Spike doesn't get the same vibe from Lou as I do. I'm starting to think she might be really lonely, and I want to make sure she's okay.

'I don't know … she doesn't seem to have a lot of friends …' I'm looking around at the crowd and I must have my worried face on.

'You have her number, so call her. But she's probably just in the bathroom or stepped outside for a smoke or something. She'll be fine. Don't let it stop you having a good time.' Spike seems really insistent that I enjoy this gig.

He was insistent I be here too. Maybe Lily's right.

'Okay, I'll send her a message.' I give him a cheesy thumbs up, but stay close to his desk for the rest of the gig.

Lou doesn't return.

eight

I wake in the eerie quiet of the house. I've hardly seen my other housemate Izzy since I moved in. She's busy at uni and isn't home much. And Lou ... I haven't seen Lou for days.

At the Roxy gig, when she didn't reply to my texts, I gave her a call, which also went unanswered. I didn't really enjoy the gig after that, but I hung around waiting for Spike. I had no idea what to do about Lou. Mel was with a bunch of people near the bar and said she hadn't seen Lou since we first arrived. No one seemed to know who her other friends were. It seemed futile to wander the city streets calling her name. Maybe she'd gone to another gig with a group of faithful girlfriends.

After the gig, Spike walked me home.

Lou wasn't in her room, so we waited up for a bit, drinking tea and chatting and worrying.

I told Spike my recent thoughts about Lou. 'I never see her with anyone other than us and she talks up her friendships in a weird kind of way. Shaun said she gives the impression she knows everyone, but does she really? Who? I think she might be really lonely. Maybe that's why she latched onto me.'

'She's never seemed lonely to me. She's so friendly and bubbly,' Spike rebutted. 'Did you ever think she "latched onto you" (as you put it) because she thought *you* might be lonely?' His defensiveness took me by surprise.

'Well ... I guess she'd be right. I have been lonely. It's harder here than I thought it was going to be.' Was I just projecting my feelings onto Lou? Maybe everyone can see I'm destined to be a loner, and not in a romantic folk-singer way.

'It's nice you have Lou as a friend, but do you think you might be making this into something bigger?' Spike continued, hesitant, 'I mean ... you do have a bit of a history of ... trying to fix everyone else's problems?' He flinched a little as he said it, as if I might slap him for pointing this out.

'I like that I care about other people.'

'I do too. I'm just suggesting you make sure you care about your own needs too.'

Spike didn't stay much longer, but we agreed we'd get in touch as soon as we heard from Lou.

I was fully expecting to hear from her by morning, but that was two days ago. I've spent those two days working and hovering by my phone. I don't know how to get in touch with Lou's parents, and no one else I've asked seems to know. I've told everyone I know that she hasn't come home. I'm hoping word will spread and maybe she'll hear that I'm worried and get in touch. I feel so helpless. Maybe I should have reported her missing to the police?

Telling everyone included breaking my silence with Taylor. I called him and he answered after the briefest of rings. He didn't mention my midnight departure from his couch. I wonder if he'd been surprised by my absence in the morning. Maybe not. I told him Lou was missing – he doesn't know her, but was worried on my behalf – and, despite myself, I asked if he wanted to hang out. He agreed to meet me at Vinyl at the end of my shift tomorrow. And he said he'd been thinking about me. What does that mean?

I'm reading in the lounge when Izzy gets home and I jump at the sound of the door. We're both a little shocked to see each other.

'Any news about Lou?' she asks.

I shake my head.

'I've been spreading the word online,' she says. 'My post got a lot of shares, but nothing useful yet. She wasn't working, so it's not like there's anyone who was expecting her to show up for a shift.'

I wonder what would happen if I suddenly stopped answering my phone and turning up to work. Who would notice? This is a big city and everyone's so wrapped up in themselves – it might be easy to just disappear.

'It's time to call the police, don't you think? I kind of feel responsible.'

'Paige?' I prepare myself for a harsh truth. 'Lou's not your responsibility. It's not your fault if she's gone walkabout. I can make the call to the police if you like. Just give me a couple more details about the night at Roxy and I'll pass them on. Then maybe we can get some sleep. Someone will find her.'

It's not my usual style to delegate responsibility, but I remember what Spike said about looking after myself. 'Thanks, Izzy.'

'It's fine. You know, a different person might be annoyed with Lou for ditching you and disappearing without a word. You're a good human, Paige. Even if you keep stealing my bread.'

I blush and start to apologise but Izzy just smiles and says goodnight.

*

'So, what do you think? A mighty excellent proposal, no?' Taylor's sitting on a stool next to me in the café window. He's turned to face me, elbow resting on the bar, fingers twitching, knee jiggling excitedly. He's just offered me a place in his band, Agent Smith. It was the last thing I was expecting.

'You know I've been dying to find a band! You guys rocked at the Goldlust gig.'

'You rocked *with* Goldlust. That's why we want you. You've already passed the audition, since we all saw you play that night. Gig's yours if you want it, Paige. Our erstwhile bass player has a one-way ticket to Europe, so the spot's a sure thing if you want it.' He grins at me, knee still jiggling. 'If you want it.' He says it for the third time, raising one eyebrow.

As if I don't.

'I would be completely honoured. Thank you!' It starts to sink in, 'Oh my god, I have a band! I mean, I can't believe it took so long, but I'm so excited! And a bit relieved.' I reach out to give Taylor a thank-you hug. I end up falling off the stool and kind of grabbing at his outstretched arms. Awkward.

I call to Caz, who's working at the coffee machine, 'Caz! I'm in a band!' It's such a dorky thing to yell across a hip café in a suburb with more bands than it knows what to do with, but I'm an excited dork right now.

Taylor gives me a high-five as Caz calls back, 'Yes!! You rock, girl!' Then she taps her watch sternly. I wave it away.

'Celebrations aside, there's the serious stuff, Paige.' Taylor regains some formality. 'We have rehearsal on Sunday afternoon – we try and make that a regular thing, and usually a few extras leading up to a gig. And ...' he checks something on his phone. 'Yeah, we have a gig booked next weekend, so that means practices during this week. Let me know your shifts and we'll work around them. It's important you come to all the practices since you don't know our *oeuvre*.' He pronounces two syllables in *oeuvre*, which I'm not sure is right. He's being a tad officious, but I take it in my stride. Actually, I feel grateful that Taylor and I met *after* he heard me play. I hate having to prove that I really am a musician to the arrogant guys who tend to dominate the band scene. I like Taylor, he's generous and fun, but arrogance is definitely part of his thing.

'I certainly intend to master your *oeuvre* expeditiously,' I say as I pretend to curtsey. I get a light punch in the arm in return.

*

I'm staring through the doorway at Lou's room. It's so her – the large mirror, the extensive collection of beauty products on the shelf. There are a few books, cute lamps and piles of clothes on the floor – mostly the ones she discarded before we went out. Because of that prolonged getting dressed exercise, I was able to describe in detail what she was wearing when I last saw her.

Izzy spoke to the police, and I had to go and file a report in person at the police station. It was incredibly anxiety-inducing. They asked me so many questions I couldn't answer, and I realised how little I actually know about Lou. Girlfriends? Boyfriends? Exes? Enemies? I have no idea. A few more pieces of the puzzle were discovered when someone reported seeing her leave Roxy, not long before I realised she was gone. She was heading into the city, apparently, and made a couple of calls before I tried and failed to get hold of her that night. Someone knows where she is. And it's not me.

I've resisted telling Dad what's going on. It seems too much like some kind of horror scenario he would have imagined happening to me on my arrival here and I don't want to give any validity to Dad's runaway imagination.

Oh, the things we keep secret from each other for fear of inducing feelings we can't handle. What secrets has Lou has been hiding, I wonder? Maybe I'm not important enough in her life for her to tell me, but the more she stays away, the more important she feels to me.

I gently shut the door to her room and go back to my own. I have a big day tomorrow. I need sleep.

*

We're gathered around the drum kit as our drummer Max twirls the wingnuts on his cymbal stands and shuffles himself into position. He was the last to arrive and is telling the long story he started as soon as he entered the practice room. It's a good story and we're captivated. He was on the tram with his cymbals and sticks, standing by the door with his gear, absorbed in his phone and thinking happily about this practice. He had forgotten his Myki, so he hadn't tapped on, and it turns out there are undercover agents on trams who are seated there looking as if they're commuting but are secretly watching for people taking advantage of the trusting 'tapping on' policy and travelling in the state's fine carriages for free. (I was never planning to skip tapping on, but this story completely convinced me and now I shall always top up my Myki and always tap on. Always and forever.) Anyway, after our impoverished and gear-laden drummer had been standing there for a while, feeling like things were going his way and thinking what a nice afternoon it was, the tram stopped and three of these incognito fare enforcers leapt up, flashed their badges and demanded to see everyone's Mykis. In an instant, a guy who was sitting behind Max jumped up and ran, prompting the three burly officials to run after him. Our drummer was saved, but spooked, so he got off and walked the rest of the way here with his gear. Hence his lateness. Hence the story, which he told with arms flailing and legs kick-pedalling.

'It would be cool if the guy who jumped off was actually innocent and was just causing a diversion. Imagine if he was just saving you! You kind of owe him,' I ponder, fiddling with my already-tuned strings. I was here on time and have been ready for ages.

'I've heard of people doing that! Taking one for the team. They are the true heroes.'

'Martyrs even.' We all take a moment as if silently acknowledging the unsung heroes of public transport, before laughing it off and getting on with what we're here to do.

'Anyway,' Taylor starts. 'We've all met Paige and are stoked she's joining us.' A vague but well-intentioned cheer spreads around the room. 'We're opening for The Dale Coopers this weekend so after this we need to set up another time to practice during the week.'

'I'm busy Wednesdays,' Nate pipes up.

'I'm free all week,' says Max.

'Cool, but we'll discuss it *after* practice. For now, let's get going.'

I admire Taylor's chairing skills, but I like him better when he's not so bossy.

There's some argument about which song to start with – they're all new to me, so I just watch as the members of Agent Smith pout and whine. Max eventually suggests a song he thinks would be easiest for me to pick up and we go with that. Taylor's on guitar and gives me a quick impression of what the bass line should be doing. It's in C major so pretty straightforward, with a standard C, Am, F, G progression in 4/4. I hold back for the first few bars just playing the root, third and fifth note. I don't want to come across like a pretentious jerk on my first practice, but I can do better than this. I'm enjoying grooving along anyway.

Taylor has a lot of solos and Max really puts his back into his drumming. It's fun music. Is this surf-rock, too? A 1960s vibe. The lead guitarist Nate also sings, mixing sweet melodic moments with a bit of raw emotion. I see potential for some backup harmonies, but again, I keep my input low since it's my first practice.

Most musicians I've met here have actually studied music. I'm impressed at their dedication, but I kind of think that if you truly love playing and you practise and listen and throw yourself into it, what more could you possibly be taught? Some genres have rules and jazz musicians need a certain amount of training, but I learnt the basics from Mr Shaw at high school and, despite his lackadaisical approach, he knew his stuff. I like to think I know what I need to.

'Nice!' Nate exclaims, 'You picked that up fast, Paige!'

'Thanks! It's a cool tune. I really like it – I'd like to play around with the bass part when I know it a bit better, maybe.' I'm not going to play lame lines to back up someone else's musical vision forever. I have vision too, you know. I moved here to work and create and play and get better.

I'm building a defence in my head when he replies, 'That would be excellent. You're the bass player. Our last guy liked to keep things simple, but whatever you think you can add is fine by me.'

'Ace.' I grin. 'Do you have any recordings I can play along to?'

'Heaps! I'll send you some links.' He gets his phone out as if about to send them to me right now.

'Later,' Taylor says. 'Let's keep going.'

I've only been privy to a few different bands' practice dynamics, but it amuses me that they usually fit into a template. There's always someone who takes control, someone who mucks about and someone who just patiently gets on with it. (To be fair, I've probably been all of those someones at some point.) Although no one here mucks around the way Jay used to in Vox Pop practices. Those were fun times in a lot of ways, but highly frustrating in others. It's good to see this more professional approach to practice.

The next song trips me up a bit. The timing feels all over the place and no matter how simply it's described to me it just doesn't make sense. I wait it out for a few bars. I don't want to seem frustrated or as if I'm criticising the song, but something about it is totally off. Regardless, I endure it and we play it through a couple more times. By the end, I think I'm getting it, but am not convinced it's a finished song. In Mudwiggle we all had a lot of creative input. I wrote lyrics and melodies and basslines. I would never dream of telling any of the drummers I've played with how to hit their skins, but otherwise I feel pretty confident that my instincts are good. I tell myself to be patient. I can build in the more technical and creative aspects that I love about playing bass. All in good time.

*

Spike's at my front door. I have a sudden flashback to the day, two years ago, that he turned up with the news about Ed's motorbike accident. My stomach drops.

'Spike. What's happened? Are you okay?' He looks older than usual. Serious.

'Yeah. Yeah, I'm okay. Can I come in?' he asks, coming in and heading for the lounge. Of course, he knows his way around. He's been here before. Before I moved in.

'Of course, come in.' I shut the door and follow him.

I put the kettle on as a reflex action to having a visitor, then sit in the lounge with Spike. His usual enthusiasm is nowhere to be seen.

'Paige, I have to tell you something. About Lou. I … I don't know why I haven't already told you. I should have said.' Spike hasn't always been good at saying what he's feeling. I'm actually impressed he's attempting it unprompted.

'Is Lou okay? You've heard from her?' I'm leaning forward demanding he continue, but not giving him the chance to. 'Sorry. You go.'

'I haven't heard from her. Not since that night. But I think I might know why she took off and why she hasn't been answering your calls.' He's been looking down at his hands in his lap, and now he looks up. I feel myself preparing to be annoyed at him for something, but I calmly let him confess in his own time.

'We – Lou and I – we've kind of been seeing each other. Casually, I guess, on and off for a while.' He looks down again. 'She's fun – good company. But I guess I wasn't feeling so into it since you got here and I haven't been as ... available to her. That night at Roxy, she was flirting with me at the desk while you were up the front. She asked me to go home with her afterwards and I said I couldn't. I was trying to work, but she said it was something else – I don't know, something about you. Then she took off. I'm sorry I didn't tell you.'

'But I asked you if you'd seen her. I specifically came over and asked you if you'd seen her because I was worried.' I'm outraged.

'I know. I lied. I really did think she had just gone to let off some steam or something. I'm so sorry. I should have told you, but I didn't know how to say it – that she was pissed off with me because she thinks I have feelings for you? How could I explain that?'

'Well, just like that would have done it.' I feel a wall come up between Spike and me. Distance is being created without either of us moving.

'I just thought she'd calm down and come back. I

thought she'd answer your messages. She wasn't mad at you.' He puts his head in his hands.

I do feel a bit sorry for him, but he really shouldn't have lied to me. 'We called the police! I've been so worried!'

'I have too! I don't know where she is, Paige. It's not like I'm not telling you that I've been hiding her this whole time. I just wanted you to know why she might have taken off. She was maybe a bit embarrassed about being turned down.'

'Gee, flatter yourself,' I say sarcastically.

He blushes.

'Sorry, but I knew there was something weird between the two of you. I was really trying to make an effort with Lou. I should have just trusted my instincts and kept out of it. Why on earth did she invite me to move in here with her? And join her band? Was she trying to keep her enemies closer or something?' I feel crushed. How to lose all your friends in one fell swoop.

'I don't know why. I really thought you two would be good friends.'

'I don't want to be friends with your crazy casual girlfriend!' I yell. We're both shocked at my outburst.

'This is pointless.' Spike gets up to leave, shaking his head, not even looking at me.

'Wait. I'm sorry I lost it.' I feel tears coming on. 'But this has been really hard for me, you know? Lou going missing – I thought it was my fault. And being in Melbourne is harder than I thought. I just wanted ...'

Spike sits down again. Maybe he really does care about me. But why does he find it so hard to tell me the truth?

'You just wanted ...?' he prompts.

'I don't know. I just wanted this to be my great moment, you know? I wanted to move here and spend time with you and play. I wanted this to be better than what I left behind.' When I say it out loud it sounds so sad I start crying. At least I'm being honest.

Spike puts his arm around me. 'It's okay if you're mad at me. I'm sorry I haven't been a very good friend since you arrived.'

The only thing this really changes is that Lou is probably deliberately not responding to my calls. She might still be okay. It doesn't change the fact that she hasn't been home for a week. I'm still worried, but now I'm also annoyed – at her and at Spike.

'I care about you, Paige. It's just ... everything's so complicated for me here. I'm so glad you're here, but I can't make any promises to you right now.'

I shake his arm off me. I feel like I've been dumped. I feel like curling up in this chair and crying until I can't cry anymore.

It's not just Spike, it's everything. I want to go home. I want Lily, I want Rose, I want Dad. I even want my mum.

nine

Ilie awake running the gamut. I'm sad, lonely, angry, worried – not unfamiliar feelings, but I didn't expect them from this adventure. I was so determined to make things work here and so convinced that this was the change I needed. After so many break-ups, disbandings, people leaving town and people getting sick, I thought it must be time for something good to happen to me. I can't believe the one friend I (reluctantly) made here has abandoned me. There must be a reason why people always leave me. Once they get to know me, once they start spending time with me, they realise they can't stand to be around me. Even Spike who knows me best of all and admits he cares about me 'can't make me any promises' – whatever that's supposed to mean. I wanted to be the one to leave this time, but my curse has followed me here. I'm destined to be left.

I look at my pathetic pile of possessions. *Chronicles: Volume One, Blue, Wish You Were Here.* What a joke. Spike never wished I was here. I've been reading too much into all of this. Dylan's enticingly titled memoir *Volume One,* as if there's more to come, as if his life is chronicled as a collectable set of encyclopaedias. I thought it was a guidebook for my life, but it's been fifteen years without a sequel – Dylan probably never intended to write one. And who do I think I am comparing myself to Bob Dylan anyway? His journey is nothing like mine. And don't get me started on Joni Mitchell.

I nearly put that album on to punish myself, but instead I flick to the more familiar *Blood on the Tracks*. I'm not quite ready to give up on Dylan. I fall asleep to him crooning 'You're a big girl now'.

*

I'm woken by my phone.

I feel a bit better than I did in the middle of the night and the thoughts that seemed so real in the dark have dissipated somewhat with the sunrise. I wish I could trust this would happen when I'm lying there awake in the night. 'Thoughts are not facts,' Molly once said to me. It's something she learned as part of her recovery. Sometimes I forget, but thoughts are not facts – especially those that emerge at 3am.

I can't handle answering my phone. It's Dad and I feel bad for letting it ring out, but I don't want him to know I'm in this state. I don't want him to worry.

I start tapping out a message to Lou. I delete and rewrite it several times. I need her to know I wasn't with Spike, that I didn't know about her feelings for him and would never go behind her back like that. But I can't figure out how to phrase it.

Spike only just told me ... I start, trying to place the blame back on him. I remember yesterday's conversation and his rejection and I feel terrible all over again.

I do have feelings for Spike. I don't blame Lou for noticing that and feeling bad, but I do blame her for insisting we be friends, then disappearing.

Dad leaves a voice message. He's checking I'm okay and I feel so guilty. I know he needs me to be okay, but I'm just not right now. I will be though. I have to be. I'm not wasting my time here moping. Besides, I have a gig with Agent Smith coming up and I talked up my ability to write a cool bass part for those slightly lame songs.

I'm in a bad unfair mood.

I decide to send the text to Lou after I've thrown myself into some melodic basslines. I can only fix one thing at a time and first I want to fix these songs. I plug my amp in and turn it right up.

*

'I just gave you my order. I'd like a flat white, please.'

Oh god, not this again. Caz and I look nothing alike! She's twice my age, for a start. Do we need to start wearing name badges?

This customer is patient and looks at me kindly. 'Are you okay?' she asks.

I blink slowly. With rising horror, I realise she's right, I did take her order already.

I actually am going crazy.

I apologise and head back to the counter to write down her order ... a latte? How can I have forgotten again already? What's wrong with me? I can feel my eyes heavy in their sockets.

'Paige, are you okay?' Caz asks. Her voice sounds like it's coming from the end of a tunnel. 'Christ, girl. You look dreadful.'

If I just collapsed here, would someone else just deal with everything for me? That would be nice. Someone else could pick me up and carry me to my bed. Someone – anyone – could decide what I should do next. I'm so tired. I can't make another decision or another movement – apart from this oddly rhythmic swaying that I've just started, I'm done.

'Paige?' Caz has her hand on my shoulder now and a

look of genuine concern.

'I'm sorry, I'm just so tired. I don't think I'm coping.' Now I feel like weeping for some reason.

'Go take a seat out back. It's okay. Have you been getting any sleep? What have you been doing to yourself?'

'I haven't slept in days. Nights. Weeks. I don't even know.' I am weeping now. I am pathetic. Am I seriously not coping with the basic fundamental aspects of staying alive?

'Lie down out the back for a bit, we'll be all right out here without you. If you feel better in twenty minutes or so you can come back, but no pressure. We can't have you collapsing on the job.'

Or losing it. I think I'm losing it.

Despite it being the world's lumpiest couch, covered in empty supply boxes and smelling vaguely of fish, I lie down and feel myself drifting off immediately. I'm in that strange state where you're aware you're falling asleep but can't tell the difference between your conscious and unconscious brain. It's blissful.

ten

I'm staring at a ghost. Facing something supernatural. I can't believe it.

She's curled up in her bed, asleep and breathing heavily. I pull her bedroom door shut feeling livid, incredulous ... and relieved.

I feel almost completely okay again, as if all the things that have been too hard recently were fuelled by this one horrible situation. In fact, it's infuriating how easily it's been resolved given the stress it put on my entire life. Suddenly everything else seems completely manageable as long as I no longer have to wonder where Lou is.

She's right here.

I call Spike straight away.

'Thank god. That's such a relief.' I can hear the strain lifting off him, but I can hear something else too. He genuinely cares about Lou.

I muster my newfound energy. 'It is, right? Hey, I think I'm going to give you guys a bit of space for a while.' My heart sinks as I say it, but I soldier on. 'I don't want to get in the way and to be honest, although I'm glad she's okay, what she did is pretty fucked. Who does that? It's attention-seeking and immature. I sent her this lengthy, wordy, grovelly text message and now she comes home? I've been so stressed, not sleeping, feeling guilty. And you lying to me about it just made everything harder. I can't be bothered with any of this.'

'Are you saying you don't want to be friends anymore?' He sounds playful but I can hear he's hurt.

'I'm saying I want you to sort it out. I wanted to come here and hang out with you, Spike. But this is not my mess. "Not my circus. Not my monkeys." So, talk to Lou, figure out what you want and ... then let me know.' Yes, I came here for the music, but I also came here because Spike was here, and I'm not going to go out of my way to make Lou feel better about herself. I've done nothing wrong here. And I'm not waiting around for another disaster before Spike tells me how he feels about me. This was supposed to be my fresh start.

'Don't you disappear on me, Paige. I don't want to lose you.'

I've never heard him sound like this before. What's going on with him?

'I don't want to lose you either, so sort it out, Spike. I'm pretty busy with work and Agent Smith right now, so take some time. Talk to Lou.' I end the call and dial another number. Dad.

*

I haven't been rostered for a shift at Vinyl since my meltdown. Rob assures me they're not holding it against me, it's just not that busy at the moment. I'm not sure what I'll do went rent is due.

At least I have my band. Agent Smith has a pretty good following, and I can't believe how many gigs we have booked. There's one almost every week for the next few months and although the gigs we've played have varied wildly in attendance and success, it's a dream come true to perform so regularly. Well, almost. The band take it pretty seriously, while still managing to celebrate in the time between soundcheck and our performance – with cheap Asian food and shots of whisky. Taylor is particularly good at negotiating a good rider for the band, so we sometimes get free food and drinks at the venue, but often that means we won't be paid for the gig.

Right now, we're in the middle of the post-soundcheck and pre-doors opening party. Max and Nate are laying into the booze and talking loudly. Taylor and I are chatting to the other band and I'm wheeling out my tried and true line about why I don't like getting smashed before a performance.

'Did you have a bad experience? I mean we've all been there, right?' Darcy's band is called Phallacy. All the members are female, and they completely wowed me at soundcheck. They're fierce, talented and smart.

'I've done some silly things.' I flash a quick look at Taylor, although we've never spoken about the night I fled from his couch. 'One time I messed up an important performance – my band was not impressed with me. I was already the odd one out – young and female in a group of older guys.' I shake my head at the memory. It was a Mudwiggle gig. We'd been asked to open for one of Will's favourite bands from out of town and it was such a big deal. I don't really know how it happened, I guess I was trying to keep up with the others (drink-wise, I mean. I was much better at keeping up with them rhythm-wise). When we got on stage, I tried to muster my most sober self, but I kept fumbling the wrong notes and losing the beat. The crowd didn't seem to notice, but it only took the briefest of disapproving looks from Will to make me feel like absolute shit. That was when I made my no-booze rule.

'When I drink, it's so much harder to play as well as I want to.'

'I respect that,' Darcy says. 'I mean, I don't abide by

that rule myself, but I totally respect it. To be honest, I have the opposite problem. I get so nervous I need a couple before I go on stage.'

Another reason to stick to my guns. May I never be someone who 'needs' a drink to do what I love.

'You get nervous?' I ask. 'You looked completely and utterly in control just now at soundcheck.'

'Oh, well thank you. It's easier when the room's practically empty. Once I'm up there, I can look in control and the music takes over, but before I go on – Jesus, I'll be freaking out backstage.' Darcy chuckles and the rest of the band nods in agreement.

'I always think a bit of nerves is actually kind of good,' Taylor says. 'It means you care about what you're doing. It matters to you. God help us all the day we feel complacent about playing to a room full of people. That would be the day to quit, I reckon.'

'Hear, hear!' I add and raise my glass of water in a group toast. 'May we always feel nervous. To freaking out backstage!'

'To freaking out backstage!' We clink our glasses together.

*

I do a double take as I walk in. Lou's sitting at the kitchen table. She's engrossed in her phone, but physically present for the first time in ages.

'Hi!' I say, a little chirpier than I actually feel towards her. She repeats my greeting but doesn't look up. Anger surges through me and I stare at her for a minute, giving her the opportunity to check herself and respond properly. She's been missing, then sleeping for ten days. I've been worrying about whether she's okay and now she doesn't even look up when I enter the room.

When she continues to ignore me, I turn and go back to my bedroom, unable to stifle a disgusted 'Wow' as I pass. Just, wow.

I lie on my bed fuming, then ask myself, WWDD? (What would Dylan do?) And I get out my notebook. It's been a while but as soon as I pick up a pen all the emotions of the last few weeks begin churning and swirling and I start writing furiously.

Pushed into smaller rooms on borrowed beds
while you bow your head
but not in shame
it's a shame all right, you choose to shut me out
refuse to let me care.

For days the room across the hall awaited your return
from your childish sojourn
your run from home
some home all right, you choose to shut me out
refuse to let me near.

I look upon this mess – not mine, I look around this
room – not mine

This town has taken much from me
and thrown the darkness in my face, in return
on your childish sojourn
did you think of me or him?
Did you want the weight of worry
to wear us all so thin?

*

Day after day we live our lives separately, Lou entering

the kitchen as I leave. If I come in while she's there, she quickly scurries back to her bedroom. It's amusing at first, so childish and manipulative, like a game. I wonder what would happen if I pretended like I was going into my room, but instead turned up in the lounge at the same time as her. I could just stand there, watching her fluster about and try to avoid eye contact. It's honestly more of a hassle for her than it is for me, so I don't care if she has to go out of her way to avoid me. But it is a terrible way to live with someone. With each passing day, I start feeling more hurt and lonely. I've done nothing wrong, but even if I had, I would expect to be given the chance to apologise or explain myself. Being ignored is awful. Lou is descending the ranks of my estimation at an alarming rate.

When I finally get rostered on at work, I tell Caz about it.

'Really? That's ridiculous,' she says. It's quiet in the café and we're sitting out the back. 'You know what you should do?'

'Move?' I say.

'No. You should get completely drunk together. Utterly. I'm talking knock-on-her-bedroom-door-with-a-bottle-of-whisky-and-refuse-to-leave-until-it's-empty drunk. That will sort things out. You'll laugh and cry and fight and get whatever out in the open. Then if you still can't see eye to eye ... yeah, then you move out.'

I laugh. 'That is so not going to happen. Aside from the fact that last time we were drinking together was when she went AWOL for a week, this is not my mess to clean up. I don't have the energy to try and fix this. I messaged her my side of it and I told Spike I'm backing off. It's like something from primary school. I think I'm going to move out.' But the thought of moving again makes me feel exhausted and rejected and useless. Struggling with the basics again.

'Fair enough. You don't owe her anything. Heck, you don't owe anyone anything! Isn't that the most liberating realisation in the world? I remind myself of it every now and then and just think, fuck yes!' Caz is grinning and I can see what she means. I came here on my own and I can make it here on my own, however I want.

'Fuck yes!' I yell, perhaps a little too loudly, as our first customer of the late afternoon arrives.

*

There's something weird going on when I arrive at the room we use for band practice. I check the time, day – I haven't got it wrong. I check for a message from Taylor, Max or Nate. Nothing. We've been practising on Sunday afternoons for weeks now and although there's a lax attitude towards punctuality, there's usually someone else here when I arrive. Today the door's locked and I'm out in the cold. It actually is cold too. The weather has turned and I've acclimatised, so what would have been a balmy barefoot 20 degrees in Wellington is now a shivering-in-an-op-shop-jumper 20 degrees here. I do a quick walk around the building to see if there are any signs of life. I find more locked doors, an abandoned vacuum cleaner, a broken table and some graffiti that looks new. So I send a text to Taylor and sit down on the front step, waiting for a reply.

It's been good playing with these guys. They're crazy good musicians and they get away with a lot because of it. I was a little nervous about the dynamic between Taylor and me since we shared some intimate moments when we first met, but it's been fine and I'm just going with the flow. Anyway, intimate moments are not to be sneezed at when they come along. Max and Nate have been perfectly welcoming and friendly, but I would never hang out with either of them outside of band hours.

What with Lou not speaking to me, me distancing myself from Spike, and money tighter than ever, Agent Smith feels like all I've got. I try to shake that thought away but can't find anything to replace it with.

Taylor replies at last. *No practice. Max and Nate at music fest this weekend. Thought I told you! Come round to mine and we can jam x*

He did not tell me, but I haul myself off the step and head back to the tram stop. A jam with Taylor sounds fun.

*

Taylor's dressed in trackies and a hoodie, looking like someone from high school. He isn't even wearing shoes. When he lets me in, his normally bustling house feels big and cold and empty.

'Where is everyone?' I ask, putting my bass down in the living room.

'Everyone's gone to Golden Plains this weekend,' he declares. 'I have the place to myself so I'm wearing my scruffiest clothes to celebrate!'

'I heard someone talking about Golden Plains at Vinyl. Why aren't you there? Why aren't I there?' I've never been to a music festival in my life, but to me it sounds loud and chaotic and utterly wonderful.

'Well, I'm not there because I have to work and would rather earn money than spend it at this point. Boring, I know. And you're not there because you have to be here to keep me company.' He grins at me.

I give him a suspicious sideways look. 'Okay ... two things. One, what are you saving for that's more exciting than Golden Plains? And two ... are you flirting with me?' I give him my sternest stare. I don't mind being flirted with, I just like to know for sure that it's happening. And I want him to know I know. It's a complicated game.

Taylor laughs, 'One, I'm saving to travel, and two, of course I am, Paige. Come on, let's make some music.'

I roll my eyes and carry my bass into the living room.

Taylor's been playing since he was a kid, mandatory guitar and piano lessons credited to what he calls 'typical Asian parents'. He writes a lot of the Agent Smith songs. He, like most musicians I've met here, also has his own on-the-side musical project and has been working on some solo recordings. He has a good voice.

In the lounge, we plug in our instruments and start with the band tunes we've been playing together. I now know these songs well enough to mess around with the basslines and add some more melody to the rhythm when it's just the two of us.

My playing has come a long way since Vox Pop. I wonder what Spike would think of my skills now. We haven't played together in years – literally. That keeps happening – I find myself thinking about Spike and what he would think of this or that, imagining his reaction and wanting to share things I see with him. I look at Taylor. He's wearing his rock musician expression and is smiling at me, nodding along with what we're playing. I'm perched on the couch I once woke up on and am plugged into a buzzing old Fender amp. I tap my foot against a table leg in lieu of Max's bass drum and let my fingers really feel the strings beneath their calloused tips, the smooth neck in my hand. We play the same tune over and over, improvising with the basic structure. I'm in the zone and realise I haven't felt this relaxed musically since I arrived in Melbourne. Gigs and practices have been great, but I'm still nervous and self-conscious playing with these accomplished musicians.

Something unsaid passes between us and the groove begins to change. I play the melody that's been in my head for the last few days and hum along. The lyrics I wrote the other day come to mind and I sing softly to myself, feeling again the emotion that inspired them in the first place. It takes me a while to realise Taylor's stopped playing and is watching me, still smiling and nodding. I catch his eye and stop, embarrassed. I've let my guard down.

'Don't stop! That's awesome. What is it?' Taylor asks.

'Sorry, I got lost in the moment there!' I make a show of clearing my throat and regaining composure.

'You did and it was great! Did you write that?'

'Yeah. It's just something I've been working on,' I admit, fingers still itching to play but silenced by my embarrassment.

'Fill me in.' Taylor starts trying out some chords and watching my fingers as I pick it up again.

Now, I'm not a singer. No one should ever have to hear me sing, but there's something compelling about this song and the lyrics are stuck fast in my memory. 'Pushed into smaller rooms on borrowed beds ...'

The bass follows the cadence of the lyrics and Taylor plays some minor chords underneath. It sounds pretty good.

'We should totally add that to our repertoire. Would you sing it with the band?'

'Oh god, no way! I mean, I'm happy for the band to play it, but I cannot sing. God no. I might have a panic attack at the thought.'

'It's okay! If you play it for Nate, I'm sure he'll sing it. Unless it's too weird. It's about your housemate, right?' Taylor's onto it.

I suppose it might be a bit much singing a song that's so obviously about Lou running off and me feeling sorry for myself about it. 'Yeah, maybe it's a bit obvious. It might not be right for a public audience.'

'It's really good though. But up to you. What else have you written? I didn't know you were a songwriter!'

'I wrote a bit for Mudwiggle, but I wouldn't exactly call myself a songwriter.'

'Well, I would.' Taylor grins. 'What else have you got?'

I start playing some other pieces I've been mucking around with, and Taylor joins in. I've mostly got basslines, but I can usually hear the drums and the lead in my head when I write. To me, bass exists within the context of a larger sound.

Time passes easily. As Taylor and I jam together, I have no idea how long I've been here. I feel like I could stay for days.

As if reading my thoughts, Taylor says, 'I could completely stay at this for hours. But I'm so hungry! And we need beer. Let's go for a walk to the shop.'

I put my bass down, get up from the saggy couch, which now feels like an old friend, and stretch and groan with the change of position.

At the store up the road, Taylor buys beer and lentil chips. I don't even pretend to offer to pay. We dance a little in the aisles to the pop songs we only ever hear in shops and taxis. Somehow we know them all with their predictable grooves, repetitive lyrics and autotuned melodies. Taylor mouths the lyrics theatrically to me. Some of them are horrifying – 'Wait, did she just say, "Tell me what you want from me I'm all yours?"' I ask, only slightly mocking my disgust.

'I believe she did. Poor thing.' Taylor shakes his head, 'We're all doomed, aren't we? I mean this kind of music is playing all over the city – all over the world even! And people are listening to it! We have a moral duty to provide thoughtful, beautiful, powerful, honest songs to fight the evil of pop music!' He grabs me by the shoulders. 'It's our duty, Paige! Our duty!'

I rally to his cry and raise a fist in the air. Then we fall about laughing, gaining some unimpressed looks from our fellow shoppers.

Taylor eyes them suspiciously and whispers to me, 'Our duty ...'

The house remains free of other people, and we continue our music-making into the night. Taylor is excellent company. Maybe he does this with everyone, but he makes me feel like the most important person in the world.

Ugh, I know I sound besotted and at risk of writing a cheesy pop song about him. I check myself and wind it back a notch.

Taylor is excellent company. Let's leave it at that.

'So.'

We've just put our instruments down and are sitting quietly in the lounge in a post-productivity glow.

I break the silence, 'So, tell me something about yourself. Why did you move here from Adelaide? What are your family like? Tell me things!' Even yesterday a question like this would have seemed intrusive, but I have a strong desire to develop this new feeling of connection with Taylor.

'Originally, I moved here to study, but it didn't work out. Adelaide's great, but the music scene is much better here. Max and Nate lured me here actually, and I've been playing with them since I arrived. My family ... well, that's a bit complicated.'

'Sounds like family,' I say, thinking of Mum mostly. I guess I've been lucky to have a pretty functional family unit.

'Yeah, well, you know how I mentioned my "typical Asian parents"? Perhaps atypically, they split up when I was in high school and my bro was nine. It was tough on everyone, but especially my mum. I miss her a lot.'

'She's in Adelaide?' I ask.

'Yeah. I visit as much as I can, but she gets kind of lonely. My brother's a bit useless, but he's there at least.'

He sounds so grown up. I've never thought about my mum getting lonely or needing to be checked on.

'What about yours?'

A couple of years ago I would have just described Dad and Linda and Rose and left it at that, but things are more complicated now. 'My mum came to visit last year for the first time in twelve years. I hadn't seen her since she left the country.' I can't imagine why I say the next thing, 'She moved back to New Zealand, but not to Wellington. The thing is ... she's really sick. She called and came to see us for the first time in ages, and then she dropped this bombshell that she's got cancer.' It feels like I've made it real by saying it aloud. I instantly want to take it back.

'Paige, that sucks. I'm so sorry.' Taylor leans forward and takes my hand. Sorry is such a funny word – when it's used in this context it always sounds wrong. It hangs there for a bit, and I resist saying 'It's not your fault' because I know that's not what he means. I'm sorry too. I spent so many years hanging up on Mum's calls and not letting her get to know me, avoiding showing any interest in her life. And now one day soon she'll be gone.

I refuse to cry in front of Taylor. Instead, I say that lie that prevents us having to show emotion, spares the other person from feeling bad and stops anyone being able to care for us: 'It's okay.'

'It's not, though, is it?' he says. 'It's horrible. It sounds completely unfair on everyone.'

'I don't really feel like talking about it.' I sound like a child, but I can't let this go any further or I'm going to lose it. Not here. Not now.

'I understand.' He gives my hand one firm squeeze and then lets it go. 'Come on, I want to play you a record I love.' And he leads me upstairs.

I wake on Taylor's couch again. This time I have full

recollection of how it happened – we were having so much fun last night, playing and talking and listening to albums, I didn't want to stop. I'm not rostered on at work today and I have slept through until morning – actually one of the best sleeps I've had in months. I smile as I take in my surroundings and the familiar visage of my bass propped in a corner of the room. I'm in no hurry to leave this morning and when Taylor comes downstairs and puts the kettle on, I still feel like my true self – my favourite self – in his company. Music is good like that.

We drink tea and chat before I head to catch the tram.

eleven

'How's the housemate situation going, Paige?' Caz asks.

Each hour I work earns a crucial portion of my monthly rent.

'No change,' I say. 'Although she did forward me a message about rent, so I guess that counts as communication.' I dump some dirty cups on the counter. 'It's like living with a ghost the way she sneaks around. I find evidence that she's been there in the rinsed dishes and the running washing machine, but she never makes herself visible. I live with a ghost.'

'We all live with ghosts,' Caz says, plummeting the conversation into metaphorical depths I wasn't prepared for.

'You reckon?' I widen my eyes at Caz but turn to a customer who has just appeared at the counter in front of me. I quickly adjust my expression and make a mental note to come back to this conversation later.

We all live with ghosts?

Caz's statement stays with me until the evening when I'm at home thinking about my actual Home. Home with a capital H. I haven't been in touch with my family much recently, but I've been trying to live by Caz's liberating statement that I don't owe anybody anything. Thinking about it now, those words sound a bit hollow. It might be liberating, but it's also isolating as hell. It's actually nice to feel connected to people and like you owe them your time and attention. And they owe you the same. It shows you care about each other. So maybe that's what makes the world spin after all. There's a fine line between what Spike said about my tendency to put others first and that selfish feeling that I only have time to look after myself. There must be more to life than this.

I don't feel like spending the evening in my room alone, so I send some messages – to Taylor, Mel and Caz. Surely something is happening in this thrumming city tonight. I'm up for anything that will prevent me from sitting here alone, writing sad messages home.

It turns out there's a party that Taylor and a bunch of others are going to. I send a quick half-hearted message to Mel and Caz to say that's where I'm going and they're welcome to join. Neither responds.

The tram ride to Taylor's is becoming familiar. I tap my Myki, hoping it's still got some credit on it and hover by the doors, enjoying bracing myself against the forward momentum, my body swaying and stopping with each acceleration. A kid near me pushes himself into the corner and disappears into his phone, unaware of his loud sniffing and the growing space around him as passengers step away from the potential germs. The seasons are changing, and I realise I'm not such a newbie to this city anymore. I live here. I ride the tram. I know where I'm going. As the days go by the strands that tied me to Wellington tug less and less often.

I arrive as Taylor and a crowd of his friends are about to leave for the party. It's a short walk away apparently. There are friends here I've never seen before, people in high-waisted jeans and jumpsuits, people wearing old band

T-shirts with shaggy hair like mine. They chatter and drink, hug and laugh around me, and seem like a tight-knit group.

'Paige is here!' Taylor announces.

No one responds, but I wasn't trying to make an entrance. He gives me a quick hug and I feel an awkwardness in my response – should I come in? Are we leaving? I stand near the door with my bag on, smiling and feeling uncomfortable, sober, boring and small.

My awkwardness eases as we walk but amplifies when we get to the party. I don't know why I'm here. Everyone falls over each other, hugging, patting each other on the back, gushing about someone's musical prowess at some recent gig. They completely ignore me.

Taylor whizzes about interacting with everyone, briefly stopping to push people in front of me who I 'should totally meet!'. I appreciate the effort, but I feel like I'll never be the kind of person someone should totally meet. These people are amazingly competent and grossly self-involved. I feel anxious and uncomfortable until I'm handed a drink and told to 'Relax, babe' by some douchebag with his hair in a bun and a gaze that drifts over my head as he hopes to be noticed by other, more interesting people.

Parties at home were always a bit lame but at least that lameness was comforting in its familiarity. We would sit around in someone's basement or living room talking about, listening to and playing music. It could get messy, but never scary – we always had a seated circle kind of vibe. We knew each other properly and talked about things we all had an opinion on. Somehow, we always had money for booze. Maybe I'm being nostalgic, but I'm sure I've never felt so out of place before in my life. People are flitting around with wide unfocussed eyes, making loud unmusical noises – guffaws of laughter and screeches of pain or pleasure (it's impossible to tell the difference). It's not until someone says it out loud that I realise what's going on. Not only am I the soberest person here, I'm also the only one not speeding out of my mind. Once I realise, it's so obvious. Everyone is completely high so it's not that they're ignoring me specifically, it's that they're just completely on their own buzz. As relieved as I am to figure this out, it doesn't make me feel any less uncomfortable. Something inside me is urging me to leave, but it's early and the idea of going back to my empty room makes me want to scream. I realise what I really wanted was another night like last time, playing music and having a laugh with Taylor, but there's no chance of that tonight. He's long gone – I mean, he's standing across the room, but he's long gone.

The sound of something breaking precedes an uproar of laughter. It's probably a bottle, just someone being clumsy, but it triggers something in me. I have to get out of here.

I go over to Taylor and try to catch his eye. 'I think I'm going to go.'

'Nooooooo!' He sounds genuinely horrified at the idea, as if this was all happening in my honour. I should have just ghosted. 'No, no, no, don't go! Do you need a drink? Stay!' He's lost his wit and articulation, but I'm glad he wants me to stay.

'I just don't know anyone. I feel out of place or something.'

'Have a drink and don't worry so much. Relax. Talk to anyone – they'd love to meet you. Here,' he stops a passing girl and demands, 'Meet Paige – she's amazing!'

The girl grins and enthusiastically hugs me hello. 'Paige! Come outside, we're watching for bats.'

I have no idea what she's talking about, but she takes my hand and drags me along with her. Taylor gives me a gentle shove and cheers as if I've accomplished something by staying somewhere I so desperately want to leave.

The outside version of the party is superior to the indoor only in that it's darker and a little calmer. 'Watching for bats' is literally watching for the bats that hang out in the park nearby. Every now and then one or two will flap past. We don't see bats in New Zealand and I have to admit they're pretty cool. There's nothing bird-like about them as they haul their leathery wings through the night sky, making a sound like shaking out a tea towel. They're a nice distraction and the air is fresh and warm. I start to feel better. Perhaps I'll stay a bit longer and see what happens. I can write a song about it later if it all turns to shit.

The music is pumping loudly now – electronic, nothing I recognise, but the bass surges through me. The drinks keep coming and the wide-eyed partygoers are dancing trance-like or slumped on couches with blissed-out expressions. Somehow, I got swept up in it, loosened by the drinks and unsatisfying conversations, and the realisation that no one's connecting with anyone here and it's not just me.

I suddenly feel exhausted and over it. Taylor insisted I stay, but I haven't seen him in ages. Why did I ignore the nagging feeling that I shouldn't be here? What was I was hoping for by hanging around? Was I expecting to have a meaningful and life-changing experience? Or was it just a way to kill a few more hours? Surely it would be better to find some like-minded people and spend my energy with them. A Courtney Barnett song comes to mind and I hum a few bars to myself – 'Nobody Really Cares if You Don't Go to the Party'.

I push my way through the crowded living room, everyone smiling just slightly above me or through me, but smiling nonetheless. They're having a good time, this is just not my scene – I need guitars and conversation. I spot

Taylor from behind and tap him on the shoulder. When he spins around, I don't recognise his expression – this is not the same charming, engaged, witty Taylor I've been hanging out with. His face changes when he sees me. 'Paige!' is all he seems able to muster.

'Taylor,' I reply. 'How are you going? I went outside for a bit then couldn't find you.'

'I've been here. Talking to ...' he gestures to the girl in front of him. She has heavy eye make-up and bright red lipstick. I hadn't even noticed her standing there.

'Emily!' she prompts, rolling her eyes.

'Emily!' he says, gazing dopily at her.

'Hi, Emily,' I put my hand out to shake hers, which feels like a perfectly reasonable response to meeting someone. 'I'm Paige.'

She looks at me like I'm an idiot. 'Right ... uh, hi.' She places the tips of her fingers against my hand in the world's lamest attempt at a handshake.

I instantly despise her.

'Are you having fun yet?' Taylor asks me.

'Um, almost. I mean, it's not my usual scene and everyone seems to be pretty ... high. But it's fun.'

'How can you not be having fun? What's wrong with you?' asks my new enemy Emily.

'I haven't been to a party like this before,' I reply, wishing I didn't sound so immature.

'Where are you from? God. You need to lighten up and live a little.' She looks me up and down and then turns away. She starts looking around the room, presumably for someone more fun to talk to.

'What a bitch.' It comes out before I can stop it and I put my hand to my mouth too late.

Emily turns back. 'What?!'

'Nothing. Shit. Sorry. I'm going to go.' I have stumbled

into a world that I was never meant to be part of. I need to leave. I look to Taylor, waiting for his support.

'Yeah, maybe you should go,' Emily says, looking me in the eye.

Taylor does nothing – doesn't stand up for me, doesn't say a word.

I give him a light push, 'Dude? What the hell?'

'Paige, go home. If you feel uncomfortable here, you should go,' he says flatly.

'You told me to stay! I wanted to go ages ago!' I'm totally blaming him for this. I just called someone a bitch and it's totally Taylor's fault. 'How do I get home from here?' I can't believe I ever thought I could be part of this scene. I am totally the kind of person who should stay at home on a Monday night. For some reason I continue, my voice whiney like a child, 'I thought we could hang out again, like last night.'

Emily's still in ear shot and I hear her snigger, her whole body shrugs with it and I can picture the smirk. I feel like such a dork.

'Paige, I'm trying to have a good time here. You're a big girl, sort it out.' Taylor walks away, leaving me to figure out how to get home – something I should probably have thought about earlier.

*

I'm standing up on the 86 tram heading to Fitzroy. It feels like the longest journey of my life. I walked for ages to find this ride and my body aches with exhaustion and irritation. The air in here is hot and smells faintly pukey. There's a woman two seats away loudly telling her life story to her uninterested seat neighbours. She's clutching a shopping bag to her chest and her eyes focus on some sorrowful middle distance. The people around her are watching her from the corners of their eyes or are turned away from her completely.

I feel sorry for her, but I'm relieved when she gets off.

The carriage fills more at each stop and I'm worried I'm not going to be able to breathe if it takes much longer. I'm swaying with the tram's momentum, my head and belly full of booze. I want to be home. Now. I want to collapse into bed and stay there for the rest of the week. What a night. And there wasn't even any good music involved.

twelve

Agent Smith has a gig at The Grand. It's going to be huge. The Grand sounds like an enormous glitzy modern awe-inspiring venue, but it's actually way better than that. It's out the back of an old pub – as so many rock venues are – all crumbling brick and worn carpet. It's epically cool and I'm stoked to be here.

Max and Nate arrive and we start to set up. After the usual greetings and gear chat, Max asks, 'Paige, what exactly happened at Emily's party? Taylor said things got a bit out of hand. Are you okay?'

'On Monday? And by the way, who the hell has a party on a Monday night?'

'You're a brave woman. I mean, even I don't go to those parties and I don't give a fuck what day of the week it is.' Max is frowning. He actually looks concerned.

Nate nods, 'It's true, he doesn't.'

'I just didn't know what sort of party it was going to be. I guess I was at a loose end and didn't feel like staying home.' My voice sounds whiney and young as if I'm explaining myself to Dad. 'Anyway, I fled in the thick of it – as I am becoming known for doing.'

'I strongly suggest staying clear of that particular group of mates. They're into some messed up shit and partying on a Monday night is the least of it. They're into some pretty heavy drugs.'

'I didn't take any drugs!' I wonder what Taylor told them.

'Good! That stuff will mess you up,' Nate says.

I can't believe it. If the two loosest guys in Melbourne are telling me to be careful, I guess I should take it as a pretty serious warning. 'I just called someone a bitch and made Taylor mad. No biggie.'

'Yeah, Emily, Taylor said. He was hoping to hook up with her and you blew it for him.' Max chuckles. I feel bad. I'm not doing so well at making friends. 'Anyway, no judgement, I just wanted to check you're okay,' Max says, tightening his drums.

'Thanks, Max. I'm okay.' Am I though?

Taylor is the last to arrive, which is unusual for him.

'Hey ...' I start, but he's in efficiency mode and breezes past me. Soundcheck should have started half an hour ago.

We play through the first tunes of our set to get the levels right. With the more melodic bass parts, the songs have filled out and Taylor and Nate play their parts together harmoniously. We're creating a cool rock sound, like proper old rock and roll. It's different to the indie-pop and garage-rock I'm used to playing, and more interesting technically, harking back to something deeper and maybe even more important than 90s grunge (though I would never tell Spike or Ed that).

The Grand is a solid place to play, and the backline and sound desk are well set up. The green room, however, is basically a corner of the pantry by the kitchen, with some drinks in a cooler for the band. We hover there for a bit, but Max and Nate want to go out to the bar. I hang back with Taylor after they leave.

I wonder when I started feeling so out of place. I have more things to connect me here now than when I first arrived, but it doesn't seem to matter.

'Hey,' I say to Taylor, not quite able to look him in the eye. 'I feel like a bit of a dork about that party.' I'm not quite ready to apologise.

'It's cool.' It's definitely not cool. Taylor's smile doesn't reach his eyes.

'I felt really uncomfortable there, but I guess I handled it badly.'

'Look,' Taylor's serious now. 'It's fine. I just don't need you clinging onto me like that. You can't run to me whenever you're feeling uncomfortable or whatever. I'm not your boyfriend. It's not my job to protect you.'

'I don't need you to protect me!' As soon as I say it, it feels like a lie.

Taylor stares at me.

I flick my fringe out of my eyes and shove my way past Taylor and out into the bar. I realise I'm pushing yet another person away. I spot Max and Nate chatting to some girls and walk on through and out to the street.

I keep walking. I'm not due on stage for another hour and a half. I'm not going to let the band down, but suddenly I need to walk and walk and walk. It's dark and I don't know exactly where I am, but I'm not too worried about finding my way back.

I wish I had made just one solid friend in this whole damn city. Someone who actually knows me, who gets me. Someone who would help me find my way home if I get lost, who would forgive me if I fucked up and who would know that a shitty drugged up electronica party with a bunch of judgemental morons was never going to be my scene.

Walking helps, but after a while, I've gone a bit far. The streets are deceptive – one minute bright and bustling, the next darkened by shadowy trees. There are eerie parks on almost every corner. I check my phone – plenty of battery life and no one's missed me yet. I decide to head back and just focus on the music. I don't need to be friends with Taylor. I just need to be able to play a few songs with him.

When I return, the bar has filled a bit more. I tell the guy on the door that I'm playing tonight and he stamps my wrist without even checking. I make a mental note in case I need to scrimp on door charges in the future.

In the green room, other bands are milling around. There's no sign of Max, Nate or Taylor.

'Hi, I'm Paige. You playing tonight?'

One of the guys has the widest grin I've ever seen. He's shaking icy water off a can of Brunswick Bitter. 'Sure are, sure are. Can't wait to get up there and rock!' He has long hair and a sparkly shirt.

I love rock musicians and their general lack of cynicism. They speak about playing with pure enthusiasm and authentic joy. Sure, there's ego in there too, but you can tell they genuinely love giving their all to a crowd.

'Me too. This venue is the best,' I say, leaning my elbow on a shelf that holds giant tins of tomatoes. 'Although it's a bit cramped back here!'

'I like it!' one of the other guys says. 'It feels … exclusive.'

I smile. These are my people. Long may the earnest enthusiasm last in us all.

On stage, Taylor either stares daggers at me or ignores me, and we're out of time for much of the first song. I do my best to stay calm and steady, but I'm irritated by the collaborative nature of this and having to rely on his whims and moods.

In a break between songs, Max whispers darkly to us, 'Sort it out, you two.' Rhythm guitarist and bass player really need to get along.

After the gig, I pack up my gear quickly. I know how to get home from here, and I don't want to have to endure a post-mortem about that completely average performance. Taylor and I will have to sort out our differences if we're going to keep playing together. I know I can rise above it, but I just don't have the energy to discuss it right now.

*

It's June. Mornings are crisp and still and the tree-lined streets are paved with the last few golden leaves. I've been working a few more shifts (thank god) and today is payday, so I'm going on a shopping mission for records. I plan the same route I took when I was job hunting (knowing now which stores to avoid) and set off on foot.

I know these streets pretty well now. I've started to recognise people – Vinyl customers, friends of housemates, fellow gig-goers and other musicians. I haven't made a BFF, but I've definitely met a lot of people. This thought makes me smile and I take off my woollen beanie, feeling warm and fuzzy.

I've spent the last few weeks with my head down. Working, practising, gigging, writing and messaging my friends and family back home, keeping things low-key in terms of going out. I really miss my family. Maybe I was wrong to think I could survive here without them. At home, everyone seems to be trucking on okay. Rose keeps suggesting I get in touch with Mum and maybe I should, but I have things here to sort out first. Dad wants me to pop back to NZ for a visit, which seems completely unreasonable. Lily and Molly are saving up to visit me here.

'I know you!' A shout snaps me from my musing. I'm on Sydney Road and it's busy. I should probably be paying attention.

'Uh ... no, I don't think so.' I flashback to the night I walked home from Taylor's. What's with people yelling at me in the street?

'I do, I know you! You're awesome.' This guy doesn't seem drunk. When I look at him properly, I think perhaps he does know me. He's dressed like Shaun, with tattooed arms and slick hair.

'I'm awesome?' I sound delighted. It's hard not to engage.

'Yeah! Bass player!' He does a quick air-bass mime in case I'm in any doubt as to what he means by 'bass player'.

I grin. 'I am a bass player. I'm Paige.'

'Paige! That's right. The lead introduced you all. Agent Smith! Keep it up, bass player!' He slaps me on the back and walks away.

Normally I hate guys in the street giving their opinion (usually about what I look like) but there was something okay about this. He was giving me a compliment on my gig. And I genuinely do like to hear what people think of my playing. It's something I work hard at.

I'm still beaming as I enter Spin Records.

'You're having a good day, I take it?' It's the older guy who informed me that no one buys records anymore. He seems to be having a better day too.

'It's going pretty well, yeah,' I reply, before burying my nose in the neatly ordered stacks. Everything I touch looks like something I should own. I'm at risk of spending all my pay.

As I wait in line to pay for my stack of records, I browse the noticeboard and its neatly pinned posters. Gigs happening, records being swapped, guitar lessons available and people looking for musicians to play with. One notice catches my eye – a folk-rock band looking for a double bass player. It's been a while, but I loved my days playing double bass in the youth orchestra. The tense rehearsals, the effort it took to get better and better at playing something that fit so beautifully into the sound of the orchestra as a whole. I note down the name and number, despite having no means of obtaining a double bass. The idea of wrapping my arms around that beast of an instrument again makes me feel warm and fuzzy again. Maybe I'm still my true self.

*

Max is smashing out a relentlessly cool beat beneath Nate's epic riffing. There's so much energy in the room today, this is the tightest practice we've had. Our songs seem to have evolved with each of our recent performances and I know them so well now I can really throw myself into playing. I've turned up my amp and gain and Taylor's grinning at me. Despite our personal differences, this is a solid band. Wordlessly, we all pause for a bar and Taylor cranks a riff into the pause before we continue, perfectly in sync on the next beat. We're all grinning at each other like idiots.

'Hey, Taylor?' I'm catching my breath as the rest of the band packs up. 'Are ... are we cool?' My bass hangs across my body and I don't want to stop playing ever. We were all so attuned to each other today.

'Yeah, mate.' He smiles for real. 'We're cool. I love having you in this band, but let's keep it about the music, shall we?'

'Sounds good to me. I love being in this band too. We rocked today!'

Too easy. I mentally check off the first repair on my list of relationships – this is a very promising start. I can't imagine Lou being this cool. She's rather more dramatic.

*

When I get home, Lou is sitting downstairs with her face in her phone, as usual. I'm still buzzing from practice so decide to be the bigger person and bite the bullet.

'Lou. Hey. Can we have a chat?'

She looks at me. Apparently, it's up to me to make the first move. I go in heart first.

'I was really upset when you disappeared. I missed you. I was worried about you. I was so relieved when you came back.' I've been rehearsing this for ages. How long has it been since she took off?

'It wasn't about you.' She speaks.

I'm so amazed at her snarkiness, I withhold my sarcastic reply. Be the bigger person, Paige. (But why is it always me that has to be the bigger person?)

'I know. I'm just trying to explain what it was like here without you. And then you come back and won't speak to me and I don't know why. It's been like living with a ghost.' I know I'm still making it about me, but I want to provoke a reaction, stop her being so damn cold. Is she even capable of empathy?

'You know nothing about my life!' she shouts. Snap.

'That's true.' I try to stay calm. 'I don't really know you at all. But we live together, Lou. We have friends in common and I was hoping we could be friends too.' I sound like that counsellor I saw a couple of times. I can see how it might work not to rise to the argument, not to raise my voice back at her.

'I just like to be alone sometimes. Properly alone. It wasn't anything to do with you,' she says, looking briefly at me and then back to fiddling with her phone in her hands.

'Okay. Sure, I get that. But what about when you came back? You don't have to tell me where you were or why you left, but I don't deserve the silent treatment.' This is what's been bothering me the most. I try so hard to do the right thing by people. It frustrates the hell out of me when others won't do the same.

'I just didn't feel like talking to you. Or to Spike. My

life is none of your business. And what's the deal with you two anyway?' She scowls at me. I guess it's a fair question.

'Spike is my friend from back home. He was my only friend here and he knows me pretty well. It was only after you disappeared that he told me there was something between the two of you. Have you spoken to him?'

'He's in love with you.' She sounds like a child calling me a name.

'He doesn't know what he wants. But we weren't deceiving you, Lou. I swear, I had no idea you two were even a thing until well after you disappeared.'

Lou rolls her eyes and flicks her phone on and then off again.

I feel like I'm talking to someone half my age, but at least we're talking at last. 'Look, I would like us to get along, but if it's too difficult for you I'll move out. I'm not prepared to live with this cold shoulder shit any longer.'

I leave her with that and head back to my room with the vague intention of searching for Housemate Wanted ads online.

thirteen

'You're welcome to come to a practice and have a listen. Can you get a double bass? Borrow one or something?' I've called the number on the folk-rock band notice and am selling myself as a double bass player, despite not actually having an instrument to play.

'I'll definitely have a look for one.' I'm scrolling through eBay as we speak, but I'll have to save quite a few paychecks to afford anything that's listed.

'Well, come meet the band anyway. Have a listen, and if it's your thing, borrow a bass and have a play with us. Then if it's still your thing – buy one!' I like this person. Her name's Maree and the band's called Virginia's Wolf, which might be the coolest band name ever.

'Sounds good. Text me the details?'

I'm excited about playing double bass again, but I'm not totally confident I can pass for a folky. Maybe if I start putting the word around my increasing collection of Melbourne contacts, someone might know someone who would loan me a double bass.

Just as I'm starting to feel back in control of my life, a figure appears in my bedroom doorway.

'Hey, Paige, I've been thinking it's time we had some rehearsals. I've written a few new songs and am booking gigs for next month.'

Was that an apology? We're suddenly all good? I'm pretty busy with Agent Smith and trying to get in with this folk band. Now Lou wants me to be her bass player again?

I swallow my irritation. I guess I can handle it. I've managed to keep things professional with Taylor despite our numerous confusing interactions. 'Oh, right. Umm, okay, if you want. It's cool with me.'

'Spike's keen and I've asked Lex to play drums. I think it'll be a cool band.'

She's more animated than I've seen her in weeks, and I would love to play with Spike again, but is this going to be really awkward? Am I even talking to Spike? Is this a completely terrible idea?

Lou's looking me in the eye and smiling. 'I mean, you've played with Spike before, so it should be a good dynamic, don't you think?'

'It sounds fun.' I don't know why I'm agreeing to this, but playing music is all I've got. Without it, I'm at risk of moping in my room forever. Or going home to Dad and his university expectations.

Maybe I can play in the band without creative input or band politics – this is Lou's project and I'm just helping her out.

'Yay!' She does a little skip. 'I'll get it organised and let you know the details.'

'Sure,' I say, but she's already elsewhere.

*

Now I'm biting another bullet. A bigger one. Breaking the silence with Lou was a piece of cake compared to this. I consider that as I type in Mum's email address.

I start and delete and start a message again. There's too much to say. I want her to know how confusing it was to have her leave when I was a kid and to then come back years later with no explanation. I want to ask her why she left in the first place, and why she came back. I want her to know it's been hard, but that I'm okay. I want to ask her how she is and I'm not sure I want to know. I want ... the messy complicatedness of a relationship with my mum.

'I was really upset when you disappeared ...' I start.

It's becoming my catchphrase.

*

I'm riding my bike along a tree-lined bike path. I ring my new bell and people step out of my way. My fingers are numb and my body is working hard to move me through this city – my city. I'm on my way to meet Virginia's Wolf.

I actually slept last night. Properly slept. After sending that email to Mum I felt lighter – in every sense of the word. The dark cloud of Mum stuff lifted, and I started to feel better. I still haven't heard from Spike, but I have a weird kind of faith in that working out too. And I love riding my bike. I'm getting myself where I need to be powered only by my own energy and simple mechanics. It's brilliant.

Virginia's Wolf rehearses in Maree's living room in Northcote. Today they're having a potluck dinner as well and I have a feeling it might be in my honour. When I arrive, I feel instantly welcome. There are four girls in the band – guitar, keys, vocals, percussion – five if they'll have me. No one is surprised to meet me and they're all there on time. (It's a musical miracle.) I'm still not sure about the genre, because my heart belongs to rock and roll, but Bob Dylan started out playing folk covers and it was his ability to do that that made him stand out from all the other James Dean, Jack Kerouac lookalikes in New York back then. (I think I read that somewhere.) Anyway, just like people are people, good music is good music. I take a seat and talk to Tess the guitarist as the plates of food are laid out on the coffee table.

'I should have brought something,' I say, embarrassed at my empty-handedness.

'No! Definitely not. We're trying to impress you, so you'll join our band,' Tess says.

After we eat, the band moves the living room furniture aside and comes into formation. The music is beautiful. More folk and less rock, but Maree on percussion and Charlie on keys add a good groove. The arrangement works harmoniously and Becca's vocals float prettily about the whole sound.

My visit ends with hugs and enthusiasm all round. I cycle home in the dark with lights flashing.

*

I try not to be offended at Rob's tone when I ask for the afternoon off. I know I'm not exactly winning him over with the short notice, but Agent Smith is playing with Goldlust tonight and I'm playing bass with both bands. Carlos couldn't play, Shaun couldn't stand in for him and I'm officially third on their list. Yay! At least there's one reliable bass player in this city. Anyway, it's going to be massive, and I need time to get ready.

Most of the people I know in Melbourne will be there tonight. I imagine my life as a complex diagram of intersecting characters, remembering that first morning when I couldn't believe the web of connections between bands and people across this city.

I'm early for soundcheck, as usual. Priorities. I haven't met this sound guy before, but he's the grumpiest yet about the lateness of the rest of Agent Smith. As usual, I reassure him they're on their way. There's not a lot more I can do here on my own, so I check some messages while I wait. I still haven't heard from Spike. Evidently, he really is too busy for me – too busy to sort out his feelings, too busy to get in touch. Lou said she'd spoken to him about the band though, so perhaps he's waiting for me to reach out? Whatever. It's starting to feel like a theme.

Mum hasn't replied to my email yet.

I mustered so much courage to write it and it felt so good putting everything down in words. Now that she hasn't bothered to reply I'm starting to feel anxious. I hate how those good feelings are so flimsy and dependent on other people doing their part. I guess I'm still glad I wrote it, and it's actually pretty typical of her not to respond. It's only been a couple of days. Or maybe she deleted it.

The members of Agent Smith all arrive at last and we do a quick soundcheck. No one ever apologises or seems to feel bad about how late they are. (Is that better than frantic and overly apologetic? I guess it wouldn't be very rock and roll.)

Soundcheck for Goldlust is straightforward and we leave our gear set up and head to the front bar to hang out. It's nice to catch up with the Goldlust guys. They've done a tour and some recording since I last played with them.

'Hey, we're going to a party back in Brunswick after we play here. You and your other band should totally come,' Tom says to me. 'Actually, that's why we needed you to stand in tonight. Carlos is playing with Radtown at a house party. I think Ghostwriters are playing there later too, so Shaun and Lex will be there. Even if we miss the bands, it should be a good vibe.' That actually does sound like a good vibe.

When I pass the invitation along to Agent Smith, Max is keen and answers for the rest of the band, 'Epic. We're there!'

*

'Hey ...' It's an apprehensive voice somewhere just behind me. Spike.

'Hey, stranger!' I say.

He looks confused by my enthusiasm. 'Enjoying the party?'

'This is an epically cool party! I was gutted to miss Ghostwriters, but how great is this place?' We're on the roof of a giant brick and concrete house, with fairy lights strung around the edge, a table of drinks to the side and a five-piece grunge band belting out tunes that sound like a *Best of the 90s* album. They can't seem to settle on a genre, but the twangy Telecaster and wailing vocals are setting the night alight.

'It's great, huh? Have you been here before?' Spike asks.

'No, I can't imagine why not though. I've clearly been hanging out with all the wrong people.'

Spike pauses. 'I've missed you, Paige.'

The band is loud and the crowd is pogoing away in front of us. I can hardly hear him, but this sounds like a conversation I won't want to miss so we shuffle to the back where we can talk.

'I'm sorry, Paige,' Spike continues. 'When you got here, things got complicated and I stuffed everything up. Now I haven't seen you in ages and I miss you even more than before you moved here.'

'I've missed you too,' I admit. 'I'm sorry too.' I think of all the things that have happened since I told Spike to leave me alone. Or did I tell him I would leave him alone? It was dumb, whatever it was.

'Do you want to go for a walk?' Spike makes it sound so serious.

'I do, but I kind of want to hear these guys play. Shall we have a bit of a boogie first?' I don't know where all my energy has come from – I've played two gigs tonight.

Spike smiles as I lead him to the dance floor. From

the roof, the lights of a police car become visible turning down the street towards us. I guess the neighbours have complained about the noise.

Spike nudges me and gestures towards the vehicles. 'Might be time to exit stage left.'

There's a small part of me that wants to see what's going to happen next, but maybe a swift exit is best. We quietly make our way down the fire escape and to the street.

*

'So, describe "complicated" to me. You've used that as an excuse twice now. Twice in three years, but still significant.'

As we walked and talked our way back to Spike's place, it felt like old times. Now, sitting in his lounge with cups of tea, sober, awake, calm and actually communicating, even the heaviest of subjects seems easy.

'I have, haven't I? Well ... I guess life is always going to be complicated.'

'It is a complicated beast,' I agree, hoping he'll explain.

'Remember when I left town – after Ed's accident, Rockfest, the end of school?'

Is Spike actually asking if I remember him leaving? Although much was left unsaid when he left, we'd connected. Properly.

'Everything ending at once like that really sucked. And I missed you heaps. I threw myself into Foldback and Mudwiggle, but nothing made me feel better.' The change had felt huge and it took me a lot to realise that it was beyond my control.

'Well, there was something else happening at the time for me too. A family thing I didn't know how to tell you about.'

'Was everyone okay? What happened?'

'My parents dropped a bombshell. I wasn't planning to leave so quickly – I was going to hang out for the summer and move up just before the start of the semester, but I couldn't deal so I took off as soon as school finished. I was more settled by the time you and Ed came to visit, but to start with I was really lonely. And I felt like me again after seeing you.'

His last sentence seems to echo around the room.

'So that year in Auckland was tough,' Spike continues. 'And the last year here has been tough too. I feel like I'm handling that stuff better now though. It feels more like home.'

'I had no idea.' I think of the Pink Floyd album he left me – *Wish You Were Here*. It was sentimental and sweet, and it had warmed me right through. I'd never thought of it as a sign that Spike was lonely. 'Your parents – what did they tell you?' I ask.

'It's like something out of the 1950s. Apparently they'd agreed to tell me when I turned eighteen. I was adopted. My parents aren't my birth parents.'

I give this a minute. I remember Spike's parents as a kind, conservative couple who looked like they had a great relationship. They stayed out of our way mostly, but when I saw them, they were usually together.

'Oh my god.' I look him in the eye. 'That is the definition of complicated.'

'Yeah. Sorry I didn't tell you sooner. You must have wondered what was up with me.'

I imagine that the secrecy would have been the biggest shock. Letting someone think for eighteen years that they're someone they're not would feel like a betrayal. I wonder if that's why Spike is so reserved. Is that why he's struggling to tell me how he feels about me or Lou?

'Anyway, it doesn't change the fact that my parents –

the ones I grew up with – gave me a good life and have always been there for me. Apparently it was my birth mother's idea not to tell me. She didn't want anything to do with me.' Now his face changes. I recognise that feeling of rejection and put my arm around him. 'She had me at seventeen and wanted to forget about me and get on with her life. I wonder how easy it was for her to forget me.'

'Seventeen! Christ. I can't imagine going through something like that.'

'I just wish she'd wanted to keep in touch from the start.'

'Maybe someone else wanted her to move on – her parents, the father ... uh, your father, I mean.'

'Whatever. I reached out to her last year and she wants to meet up – but I don't know if I can deal.'

So many thoughts and feelings are coursing through me right now – empathy for Spike's situation, but also for his birth mother. I can completely relate to being rejected by a mother – someone whose love should be unconditional – but there are always two sides to a story. I wonder what hers is.

'Mum stuff, eh?' We've only talked a little bit about my own mum, but Spike nods. He knows I get it.

'Do you know anything else about her? She's a Kiwi?' I ask.

'Yeah. Weirdly, she went to West End High. In the 90s. She got pregnant to her boyfriend in their last year of school. I looked them up – they seemed cool.'

'Well, they're your family.'

We sit in silence for a while.

'I wonder what she was like as a teenager. Like, it was the 90s. She was there when Radiohead released *The Bends*, when Kurt died, and *Melancholy and the Infinite Sadness* was played to the world for the first time.' I'm seriously excited by this thought.

'Oh, yeah!' So is Spike.

'I wonder what she listened to when she was pregnant with you. Sorry, that was a bit much.' I take it back just in case.

'No, it's okay. That's a cool thought actually. I know my parents weren't listening to anything cool when I was a baby. They were already old. Maybe she's the reason I love rock. Maybe she was a musician. I've always wondered where my passion for guitar came from. My parents are completely not musical.' He looks cheered by the possibility. 'Hey, so apparently we're in a band together!'

Somehow this had completely slipped my mind. 'Lou's band?'

'Yeah, I'll believe it when I see it.'

'You don't think it will happen?' I ask.

'Lou's been asking me to play with her for ages, but she never calls any rehearsals and keeps booking solo gigs. I'm happy to play though – hey, maybe you and I should try and make it happen?'

No way I'm stepping on Lou's toes again. They seem to be easily-stepped-on toes. 'I think we should leave the band stuff up to Lou. But you and I should have a jam – I can't believe we haven't already!' Spike and I played well together in high school. There were some terrible moments, but as time passes I find I mostly remember the really good gigs and practices, when it just felt completely right to be making music together.

'We could do that right now. Greg won't mind if you borrow his bass. I'll grab my guitar.' He leaps up. It's late, but if Spike thinks it's okay I'll go with it.

He runs back in, leaves his acoustic guitar with me then goes rummaging in Greg's gear stash to find a bass for me. I pick up the guitar and start playing. Like I said,

I know a few chords. Without even thinking about it, I'm singing my song about Lou again. It really got under my skin. I can't remember exactly how I played it with Taylor, but it seems to have developed in the time I've left it sitting. I don't notice Spike standing, watching and listening, but I stop quickly when I do. Shame.

'What was that? It's great,' he says. 'And you can totally play guitar!'

I blush a little. 'It's a song I wrote a while ago. It's full of *feelings*.'

'Keep playing.' Spike sits down with the bass he retrieved. He picks out a crude bass line, but I can hear how it might work. I've never sung in front of Spike before and I'm surprised at how self-conscious I am about it, although I do like the role reversal of him following my lead.

'You have a great voice,' he says when I've exhausted the limits of the song. He's so enthusiastic about everything, it's hard to know when he's sincere. I give him a funny look. 'No, you really do! I can't believe I've never heard you sing before. Vox Pop could've been so much better with you up the front!' He's waxing lyrical now and the compliment has gone too far.

'Yeah, but who would have played bass? Jay?' I laugh.

'That song's about your mum, right?'

I look at him blankly. He quotes my lyrics at me as explanation, '"... your run from home ... some home all right, you choose to shut me out ..." It's about your mum leaving?'

'I didn't think so as I was writing it, but maybe.'

'Unconsciously, maybe. You know ... you're struggling to fit in here in Melbourne, but other people see you at all the gigs, playing with the best bands, hanging out with cool guys like me ...'

I laugh, but I'm not entirely convinced.

'Have you thought about going solo? Singer-songwriter styles?' He actually sounds serious. 'There are loads of musicians here who have side projects – play in a band while working on their own music. It makes sense. You get a bit more control over things musically.'

'I haven't really thought it, but I have been getting a bit frustrated with band dynamics – people turning up late, playing badly, making promises they can't keep ...'

'Agent Smith not going so well?' Spike asks.

'Actually, they're awesome, but I miss having a bit more creative control. And I could definitely be a bit busier musically.'

'I reckon go solo. Either that or study sound engineering.' I don't know if Spike is taking a swipe at himself there, so I refrain from scoffing. I respect sound engineers, but I don't want to be one. And I love playing with bands, but the few times I've had a jam and played my own songs, I've felt really alive. Sort of validated and – like Spike said – in control.

'I've actually got a notebook full of songs,' I confess. 'I've been writing for years. I got to play a handful of them with Mudwiggle, but there are heaps more. I could dig them out.'

'And if you want to record a demo or something, you know where to find me. Me and Greg's gear.' Spike grins.

*

Everything's coming at once in a tsunami of musical opportunities, and I love it. Virginia's Wolf found a double bass for me to borrow and they've invited me to join the band; Lou – contrary to Spike's cynicism – has called our first rehearsal for a gig she's booked; Agent Smith is building momentum and I'm going through my notebooks practising songs I've been writing for years. And I'm writing new ones. I need to squeeze in more shifts at Vinyl, though. I foresee some pricey instrument purchases in my future.

I'm about to head to Lou's rehearsal when my phone rings and Dad's hairy face appears on my screen – it's a photo I took of him before I left. I check the time. If I stop to talk to him I'm going to be late. I'll call him back later. I jump on my bike and the wheels start to spin.

*

'Lou Key and the Loose Keys? Or maybe just ... The Loose Keys?'

'How about ... Lou Key and the Spooky ... something?'

'Lou Key's Spooky Keys.'

'These are all awful.'

'Does it have to be a Blah and The Blahs kind of name?'

Lou, Spike, Lex and I are at our first practice for Lou's band. Deciding the all-important band name has dominated the first half-hour.

'I know it sounds a bit egocentric, but I want to keep my name in it so I can still do solo shows and be recognised. That way I can play the same material with or without the band, depending on the kind of show it is.'

'So, we're dispensable?' Lex asks.

'Yes,' Lou smiles.

'Lou Key and Her Dispensable Band,' I offer.

'Lou Key and ... does it have to rhyme?'

'I feel like it ought to rhyme. Or have some play on my name.'

'Lou Key and the Chains? Like key chains?'

'Lou Key and the Locks.'

'Lou Key and the Padlocks.'

'Lou Key and the—'

'Something like ... low key ... something ...?'

'Stop! My name's starting to sound ridiculous

the more you keep saying it!' Lou tries to shut down the brainstorm, but we're unstoppable. No wonder there are so many rubbish band names in the world. The harder you try to come up with something clever, the more ridiculous it sounds.

'Lou Key and the Loo Keys – like keys to the toilet.'

I start an ironic slow clap at Lex's suggestion, 'Congratulations, that is officially the worst thing I've ever heard in my life.'

'Let's just play some music and think of names later. I'm sure a moment of brilliance will hit one of us soon. Odds are it's bound to happen.'

*

I wake to so many missed calls I don't know where to start. Dad, Linda, Rose ... This can't be good. I've slept through an entire morning of my family trying to get hold of me. I'm going to have to start scheduling time to call them, now that I'm so busy. Just as I'm dialling in to the first of fifteen new voicemails, my phone rings again. I answer in a pulse beat.

'Dad! I'm here. I've just woken up.' My urgent voice goes unanswered for a semi-quaver and I panic in the brief silence. 'Dad?'

'Paige, sweetheart, there you are. We've been trying to get hold of you. Rose is here. We've heard from your mum. There's been a change in her ... situation. I think ... I think I'll put Rose on.' He disappears before I can respond and Rose's voice takes over.

'Paige, where have you been? We've been trying to get hold of you,' she says.

Mum stuff. Just tell me.

'What is it?' Just tell me!

'Paige, Mum's in hospital – up north – and it's looking

bad.' Rose's voice breaks. 'They said we should make arrangements – go and see her.' Her voice cracks again.

'How? I don't ... Mum's sick, I know, but I can't ...' Everything on my unwritten schedule floats to the surface. I have too much happening here. I have gigs coming up. I can't just drop everything and let everyone down to run back home, for god's sake. I barely have rent money, let alone money for flights.

'Dad's going to pay for us to fly up so we can spend some time with her. You need to come home, Paige. It's important.'

Of course it is, I tell myself. Of course it's important. It's also terrifying. And it's a lot of effort to go to for someone who never made much effort for me – she never even answered my email.

'Paige?'

'I'm here,' I say. 'I don't know what to do. I know I should go with you.' I start to sob. I wish Rose were here, within reach. I wish she would put her arm around me.

'It is hard,' she says. 'It's really hard.'

I'm nodding like a child who doesn't realise they can't be seen at the other end of the phone. I have no words.

'I'm putting Dad back on for a bit, but I'm still here,' Rose says before Dad's baritone takes over again.

'Paige, love? You there?'

'I have no money.' It comes out in a teeny tiny voice.

'I'll pay for the flights, love. Don't worry. You don't have to do anything except get on the plane. I think you'll regret not seeing her.'

Once upon a time she was everything to him too.

A better person than me might ask him how he's feeling, but I still have no words.

fourteen

There's a knock on my bedroom door and I realise I've been lying here on the bed for hours, just staring at the ceiling. Was I even thinking about anything?

The knock comes again and Lou's voice calls, 'Paige? Can I come in?'

It takes me a moment and when I respond my voice is croaky. 'Come in.'

I move myself into a sitting position as Lou creeps in and shuts the door behind her. She sits on the edge of my bed and looks at me. She doesn't say anything for a long time and her silent concern starts me sobbing again.

'Did something happen? I heard you crying. Was it a call from home?'

'Yeah. My family called. I ... my mum. I have to go home and see Mum. She's in hospital. I don't want to, but I know I should.' Saying I don't want to go home to see my sick mum must sound incredibly selfish and unkind to someone who doesn't know about my complex abandonment issues.

'You don't want to see her? Or you don't want to leave here?'

'I know I sound horrible. I'm just not sure I can handle this. I was only just starting to find my feet. I have so much going on here.'

'Do you want me to call Spike? Or your work?

Everyone will understand if you have to go home for a while to deal with family stuff. I know the timing isn't great, but it sounds like something you need to do.'

How is everyone else so level-headed and mature all of a sudden? I'm such a baby, crying and whining while others are so reasonable. It must be easier when it's not about you.

'Thanks,' I say to Lou. 'I can make those calls.'

'We'll keep your room for you – there's nothing to worry about there. You'll come back and fit straight back into your life here.'

I feel so grateful right now I could cry all over again. 'Thank you,' I say, and she puts an arm around me.

*

Shaun's driving me to the airport and Spike's come for the ride.

Work gave me a couple of weeks off and Agent Smith, Virginia's Wolf, and Lou Key and the Whoever-we're-going-to-bes have all promised they'll manage without me for a little while. I won't be replaced.

I spent years not talking about Mum stuff, but now I'm realising people like it when you share things like that. It shows you trust them, and they appreciate the chance to rally around, to care and feel needed. I guess people like to feel they're helping.

I try to sleep on the flight, but I have too much on my mind and keep waking with a start. I haven't slept much since the call from home, but I'm used to running on fumes. I almost can't remember what I'm like when I'm well-rested.

The last three-quarters of an hour crawl past and I grow more and more anxious. I'm humming, and it takes a few minutes to recognise the tune as one off *Blue*. The one about a flight, set to a frenetic beat that I tap out anxiously on the armrest. I watch the animation of the plane creeping to the edge of the Tasman Sea, closer towards Wellington. The familiar shape of New Zealand on the screen gives me a strange surge of patriotic comfort.

Dad, Linda and Rose meet me at the airport. I spot Dad before he spots me and watch his expression change from scrutinising the disembarking passengers to the biggest smile of relief when he recognises me. He hugs me so tight I wonder if I'll ever be allowed to leave home again. He's organised our flights so that Rose and I will have a few days at home with him on either side of our visit to Mum. I wonder why he decided not to come with us.

Back at home, I feel like a kid again, fussed over and worried about, after months of fending for myself in a foreign country. (Well, not an entirely foreign country, and not entirely without help, but I have been managing without Linda's 'Have you got a jacket?' and Dad's 'Is that all you've eaten today?')

'So, who's Max again?' Dad asks. My family is gathered around the dining table and it feels like old times.

'Max is the drummer for Agent Smith. Lex is the drummer for Lou's band.'

'And Lou's band is called Goldlust.'

'No, Lou's band is Lou's band. We don't have a name yet. Goldlust I've only played with a couple of times, standing in for their bass player Carlos. I don't think I've mentioned the drummer from Goldlust before. His name's Tom.'

'And Virginia Woolf? How does she fit in?'

'Virginia's Wolf!' I correct. 'They're the folk-rock band I play double bass with. Their drummer is Maree, but she calls herself a percussionist. She doesn't have a full kit, but plays bass drum, chimes, glock, some cymbals ...'

My life sounds so complicated and cool when I explain it to my aging parents. Hard to keep track of all the drummers apparently.

'It sounds so busy!' Linda exclaims.

'It has its quiet moments too,' I assure her. 'It's not like being at school where every minute is scheduled out for you and there's hardly any time to yourself.' I've had far too much time to myself in the last few months.

'What about you and Spike? What's going on there?' Rose asks in a sing-song way. Why is it always about the romantic chase with her?

'Spike's good. We're good,' I say enigmatically.

'Like ... *good*, good?' she insists.

'Like ... just good.' I poke my tongue out at her.

It's the truth. I'm glad Spike and I managed to make up and get on with things. I like having him around. Am I still holding out hope for romance? Well, maybe. I was conditioned that way, wasn't I? Bloody pop songs and poetry.

After dinner I have a nostalgic rummage through my cupboard and collect some things to take back with me. My winter coat, a few CDs. I'm slowly repopulating my life with sentimental objects and adding weight to my anchor in Melbourne.

It's weird being home and not having Lily and Molly around, but I'll call them tomorrow. I know they'd have come home to see me if they didn't have exams.

*

Rose and I stay up talking into the early hours of the morning. I'm beyond tired, but there's so much to catch up on. I've missed this. I've missed her. We're lying on my old bed and it feels like the hug of a familiar friend after all the couches and borrowed beds I've endured this year. Even the bare walls of my room are comfortingly familiar.

'Have you seen Ed?' I ask Rose.

'No. I told him I was coming home and what's going on with Mum. I might try and see him, but I don't know.' Rose and Ed really made an effort to stay friends after their break-up. But their relationship was years ago now and moving on seems to be an inevitability.

'Would you mind if I went to see him? I'd love to tell him about Melbourne.'

'Why are you asking me? He's been your friend for ages.'

'I know. It just seems respectful to check.' I yawn and curl up smaller and smaller.

'Thanks for asking then.' Rose gives my shoulder a squeeze then rolls herself off the bed. 'Sleep time. See you in the morning.' She shuts the door behind her. It's the last thing I hear until daylight.

*

I'm at Tempo drinking hot chocolate with Ed. It feels like I've never left and like an entire lifetime has passed since I did. Ed has been in Wellington all this time, studying music, working and playing in two bands. Rose told me that since his motorbike accident, he still needs regular sessions with a physio, but he looks like the same old Ed to me.

'Sounds cool, Paige. How do you have time to be in all those different bands though?'

'Well, it's all I'm doing. That and working in the café. It's not like I have to fit playing around study or family. I work and play music and still find time for the odd lonesome solo in my room.'

'I like solos,' Ed says.

'I'm learning to like them too.'

'So you're heading up north tomorrow, yeah? And then how long are you around for?' He's managed to avoid the Mum word, but we both understand what 'heading up north' involves.

'I have a couple of weeks off work. Dad booked the flights, but I'm getting a bit worried he won't want me to go back. Plus, we don't know what it's going to be like ... you know ... up north.' A handy euphemism.

Ed leans back in the low chair and I think I see him wince. He looks older with his stubbly face and beanie pulled down. I think I can see more clearly now how different he and Rose are and maybe why they broke up. Although Rose does have an adventurous side, she's mostly studious and sensible. I don't even know what kind of music she listens to these days.

*

Dad looks grey as he drops us off and waits around for our flight to be called. I can tell he's trying to be jovial, but there's really no need. We are all aware of the gravity of this situation. Rose and I sit clutching our boarding passes. We're early and anxious and I just want the next four days to be over.

Suddenly someone has their hands over my eyes and a familiar voice cries, 'Paigey!'

I turn.

Lily and Molly are standing behind me waving matching boarding passes.

'What are you doing here?!' I leap from my seat to hug them. 'You have exams!'

My family are smiling conspiratorially, and Lily and Molly are beaming.

'We're coming with you!' Lily squeals.

'We won't get in your way or anything, we're just coming for moral support. And shopping,' Molly says.

'It's completely amazing to see you!' Lily throws her arms around me again and I'm overflowing with love and tears.

'What about your exams?' I ask.

'Ah, the magic of study leave. When Rose told us what was happening with your mum, we were like, duh, as if we're not going to be there for our best friend. You would – well, you *have* – done the same for us.'

'Have I?' This is the most generous gesture ever.

'Sure, you have! Anyway, we needed an excuse to escape exam prep for a bit.'

Our boarding call comes across the PA system, and I'm so thrilled to see Lily and Molly that I almost forget to say goodbye to Dad. His face seems to have lightened with the atmosphere and I rush back to give him a tight squeeze. 'See you soon.'

fifteen

'Paige. Thank you for your email. I'm sorry I wasn't able to reply, but I've been thinking a lot about what you wrote. You were right to tell me.' That's the first thing Mum says to me. Acknowledgement, validation. It's not an apology, but it's something.

'It's okay. You don't need to reply. I just wanted to tell you how I felt. You don't need to worry about it now though.' After years of wanting her to understand and apologise and feel remorse, it's suddenly the last thing I want her to do. She's already pale and puffy and sick. Properly, horribly sick.

Changing the tone completely, Rose pulls out a stack of trashy, bright magazines. 'We brought you these!'

Hospitals make me so uncomfortable. Sombre faces remind me how grim this situation is, and cheery faces are jarring. The people in this wing know they're not doing well. Our visits can't last long, but we keep going in morning after morning. Mum doesn't say much, but she seems glad we're here. It feels like visiting some distant family member. It would be easier to think of her as a great aunt or something, but she's not. She's my mum. She gave birth to me. I have no idea how Rose is able to hold it together so well.

*

Rose and I are staying with Mum's sister, sharing a room in her big house by the beach. Lily and Molly have rescued me from being stuck there again this evening.

'How's it all going?' Molly asks as the three of us wait for our food at a busy Japanese restaurant. 'With your mum, I mean.'

I'm so glad they're here. They've taken a week out of their lives to be here for me, mostly by distracting me from the drama of Mum stuff, but of course they want to know what it's been like too.

'It's tough,' I say. 'It feels like every visit is longer than I can handle, but at the same time I know it might be my only chance. I know it means a lot to her to have Rose and me there.'

'Are you getting something out of seeing her too? I mean, I know it's horrible, but is there some part of you that can enjoy your time together?' Molly asks.

'I wish. I hate the hospital. It's too quiet and bright and uncomfortable. I feel like I'm just doing this for her, and I guess I can feel proud of that, but it's tough. Remember when she visited last year?'

'When you were glad to see her, sorry to see her go, and disappointed that nothing was resolved?'

I smile. 'I'm glad you guys are here.'

'We're always here for you! We'll eat teriyaki tofu and talk about everything else in the world for you!' Lily declares. 'No quiet or bright with us, eh Mol?' She winks at Molly, who is ironically the quietest and brightest of us all.

'Do you want us to come with you next time?' Molly asks. 'We need to go back to uni in a few days, but we'll come if it would help ...?'

My friends are the best people in the world. Why did I ever leave them?

A reminder comes in the form of a message from Spike.

Heya, how's it all going? I've been thinking about you lots and hope Mum stuff is as okay as it can be. We have a sweet gig with Lou's band lined up and it would be ace if you're back for it. No pressure though. We miss you xx

*

'So why Melbourne? It seemed a shame you left New Zealand so soon after I moved back,' Mum asks me. She seems perkier today.

Rose looks at me sideways and whispers, '*Spiiiiiiike.*'

'No! I mean, Melbourne's cool. There's a great music scene and lots of people like me. There are gigs every night. I can cycle everywhere. Did you know there are over 70,000 live gigs a year in Melbourne? Anyway, all the best musicians leave their small-town homes to make it big. It's like, Melbourne is to Wellington, what New York was to Dylan's Minnesota, or Joni's Saskatoon.' I'm rambling.

Mum jumps on my Joni reference, 'Have you been listening to *Blue*?'

'A bit, but it's kind of ... sad.'

'Yes!' Her face brightens like I've never seen it. 'It's poetry, Paige. All imagery and storytelling. I mean, can't you just picture her drawing a map on a coaster by the light of a TV? And her characters, they've all got something to teach us – Carey and the boyfriend who busks in the park and likes to walk in the rain. And don't get me started on Richard!' She chuckles. 'He ends up drinking alone with all the lights on every night. He's our final lesson from that album. After all the sadness and longing, Joni's saying, don't be a cynical Richard. Stay romantic, stay vulnerable.'

'I like that song about her catching a flight,' I say. 'I like the galloping pace and she's so pragmatic. And how she integrates that "Star light, star bright" nursery rhyme into the lyrics. It's clever.'

'It's poetry! All those details, renting a piano, wanting to leave, but wanting to be part of it too. She wants to get something out of a place and then move on, but moving on isn't as easy as she thinks. What do you think about a song getting under your skin like a tattoo?'

'I don't know... I've never thought about it.'

'Sorry. I can get carried away talking about *Blue*. I'm so glad you've been enjoying it.'

I haven't really, but I smile back at her.

'Do you think you'll stay in Melbourne?' Mum asks. 'Or is this more of a gap year?'

I guess originally I pitched the idea as a gap year. I was hedging my bets. But being back here this last week or so, I've been feeling more and more out of place. It's taken a while, but I think I'm finally starting to find where I fit in Melbourne.

'I think ... I'm going to stay there.'

'Don't tell Dad!' Rose says.

'What do you mean?' As far as I knew, my future was up to me. Dad's been a bit protective, but he's not controlling.

'It's just, he's really hoping you'll come back and study. I thought you knew that.'

'I know he'd like me to do that if it doesn't work out in Melbourne, but it *is* working out. What would I study anyway? I already know how to do the only thing I want to do and I'm already doing it!'

'You mean playing music?' Mum's slow on the uptake.

'Yes, playing music!' I say defensively and too loudly.

'It's okay, Paige. Calm down,' Rose whispers and puts a hand on my shoulder as if I need restraining.

'You calm down!'

'Sounds like you do need to have a chat with your dad though, Paige.'

Suddenly my mum is full of advice?

'I think we should go,' I say childishly. Then check myself. 'Sorry, Mum. It was nice to see you today. We'll be back tomorrow.'

'We will, but tomorrow we're flying home in the afternoon,' Rose says.

'We are?'

Mum's face crumples. 'Can't you stay a bit longer?'

'I'm sorry, Mum. I have to get back to uni and Dad's booked Paige a flight back to Melbourne.'

Reluctantly, no doubt.

'I understand.'

'But we will be back here in the morning, Mum. Promise.' Rose seems to have taken on the parent role, comforting our abandoned mother. I don't think I can stand it.

*

I read this book last year about an asylum seeker and her family's harrowing journey by boat to Australia. Her waking hours were terrifying – packed into the boat with hundreds of others, with no idea where they were headed, how long it would take or if they would survive. Everyone was on high alert, stressed and seasick. But while she was asleep on the boat, this girl dreamed of her home – cooking by the fire, her school friends, the pet dog they'd left behind. Happy, comforting dreams. It was only when she and her family were safely on land and settled into a centre with dry beds and hot meals that she started having nightmares about drowning or being lost in a vast shoreless sea.

I'm thinking about this as I pack to fly home – the idea of being able to process huge changes only with some distance between you and them. Being away from Melbourne has made me realise how lucky I have been there.

The things I've wanted from the place – a band, gigs – came to me. Just as being here with Mum has lessened my fear of Mum stuff. It's been shocking to see her so unwell and totally emotionally draining, but it was actually easier than I had imagined. But then I don't know whether any amount of time with Mum would have felt like enough to resolve anything. Saying goodbye to Mum was the worst.

Lily and Molly left a few days ago, but they say they're still planning to visit me in Melbourne. Dad will meet me and Rose at arrivals in a couple of hours. We sob softly in the departure lounge, holding hands, without needing to say anything. I know Rose and I are not the first or last people to shed departure lounge tears. Airports must be covered in the tear stains of people having to leave loved ones behind.

*

'So, Dad.' After family dinner, it's time for me to have a quiet word with Dad.

'Paige, I can't believe I booked you a flight home!' he jokes. He's doing something on his laptop, but he could just be scrolling through Facebook.

'Yeah. About that. I mean, thank you for this trip. It was really hard and really important to see Mum. You were right. And it was really good to see you too.' I grin at him.

'You're welcome. Next time maybe Linda and I could come over and see you in Melbourne. I know she's been dying to check out the art galleries.'

'Sure! You should definitely visit.'

'I get the impression that's the only way I'm going to see you again. Anyway, we'd love to see you in your more natural habitat.' Classic biology reference from Science Dad.

'It does feel more natural to me there,' I say. 'I really think I'm going to stay.'

'I know.' Dad takes off his reading glasses and looks at me square on. 'I'm really glad you've found a place that suits you, Paige. You've come into your own even in the short time you've been there. And you get to play music! You love that. And so I do too, because I love you.'

'Aww.' I give him a giant hug. 'You weren't hoping I'd come back? Go to uni nearby? Live back here with you?' My words are muffled by his big jersey.

'I do worry, Paige. You're too thin, you're short of money. (I've put something in your bank account, by the way, just to keep you going.) I want you to live your life, though. And I'm proud of you.'

I give him an extra squeeze. Of course Dad wouldn't demand I come home. In your face, Rose.

PART TWO

sixteen

The house is empty, but I carry my bag up to my room and find the hugest bunch of flowers next to my bed. They're beautiful. I don't think I've ever been given flowers before in my life. (How I've gone eighteen years without such a thing is a total mystery.) My heart leaps a bit at the potentially romantic gesture, but I know they're sympathy flowers. Still, they're a welcome burst of brightness in my colourless room. I try to guess who they're from before reading the tag. *Welcome home, Paige. We missed you. Spike and Lou.* What a strange trio we are.

My phone goes crazy when I put my Australian SIM back in. It's been two weeks and I'm itching to reconnect. There's a message from Taylor checking how I am and asking if I can make it to practice this afternoon, work offering me a Monday morning shift, Virginia's Wolf with some undisclosed exciting news ... I say yes to all and pick up my bass, hugging it to me before plugging it in.

*

'Paige! I hoped I'd find you here.' Spike has wandered into Vinyl as if it's not the busiest time of day. It is the busiest time of day, but it's actually kind of quiet.

'I got the first shift I could. I need to start earning again.' I carry a latte to a table in the window then pause to chat on my way back. 'What's up?'

'I missed you! How long were you away for? Months, right?' Spike hugs me.

'Two weeks,' I laugh. 'But I missed you too. And I missed Melbourne! What's been happening? Fill me in.'

'I will leave you to your shift but come round to mine after and we'll catch up. You can tell me about Mum stuff. Or not. And I'll tell you everything I know about Melbourne stuff. We'll get takeaway and hang. Sound good?'

'Sounds excellent.' I grin at him and he hurries out again, leaving me to try and look busier than I really am.

'I missed you too,' Caz says from behind the counter.

'Aww. I know. You already said.' I smile at her.

'I did? Well in that case ... get back to work!' she orders.

I love being back. I like the way Spike pops in to invite me to things. He has my number, he could have just texted me, but there's something charming about the in-person invite – harder to say no to and more sort of cordial. And after lunch he sends me a reminder text. He's keen.

When I finish my shift, I grab my bike and head over.

Knocking on the door, I remember the first time I came here, the first time I met Lou. It was summer – hot and lazy feeling and everything had a shine of newness. Now cold rain squalls pass most days and when they don't the air is crisp and smells like ice. Tonight I'm wrapped up in my scarf, gloves and a thick jacket.

It's no warmer inside the house.

'Welcome! Our heating's broken. It's like a fridge in here.' Spike's wrapped up too and smiling apologetically. 'But wait! I got you a present.' His face lights up. 'Come in, come in.'

Spike leads me to his room where a square red suitcase sits on his bed with a big bow on it.

'What's this?' It comes out like a squeal.

'It's nothing really, but I saw it and thought of you. Open it!'

I carefully remove the bow and unclip the suitcase. It's a Victrola portable record player. A new one. The unused needle on a strong arm, poised above the pristine turntable.

'Oh my god. It's so beautiful. I love it! Thank you!' I'm fixated on the neatness of it, speakers set into the front and two simple dials.

'I thought you'd like it. It has Bluetooth, so you can hook it up to anything. Now, you know you can borrow any of my records, but I got you these essentials to go with it.' Spike hands me a short stack of vinyl and I flip through – *A Night at the Opera*, *Abbey Road*, Oasis, Smashing Pumpkins.

'Spike, this is the best, most thoughtful present I ever got.'

He shrugs, but he's beaming. 'I couldn't stand to think of you listening to Spotify on your laptop any longer.'

I give him a hug and he smells like I remember – warm and real. I hold him for ages and for the first time since I arrived here, I feel calm. This feels like home.

I'm about to say something when he lets go. 'What should we listen to first?'

We put on *Abbey Road*, gently sliding the record from its sleeve and placing it on the turntable. The needle moves over it like magic.

We listen to the entire album, the three of us – me, Spike and the Victrola – lying on his bed, occasionally singing along, until we're both starving.

*

'So I have to tell you – while you were away, Lou and I had a chat.'

My heart sinks. We're surrounded by plastic containers scraped clean of takeaway. My new red Victrola has been playing all our old favourites. I'm really not in the mood to bring Lou into this perfect evening.

I try to keep a poker face, 'How'd it go?' The broken heating means I had put my coat back on and now I wrap it a little tighter around my body.

'She said she's trying to do the right thing by you. She really wants us all to be friends.'

'She does. We are. She was lovely to me about my Mum stuff.' Have I done something wrong again?

'Yeah, well, it's all genuine. But she and I had needed to have a chat about her and me. It was hard but good, you know, and she understands and is, you know, cool with ...'

'With?' I prompt as he stalls, but I'm starting to feel annoyed. I don't want or need Lou's permission to hang out with Spike.

'Well, you know, I have ... feelings for you, Paige. I have for ages. I needed to sort things out and I've done that now, so ...'

My phone starts ringing. I thought I'd put it on silent. Terrible timing, sure, but it's Taylor and might be band stuff. I haven't talked to him since I got back. Maybe we have a gig.

'Sorry, sorry, sorry!' I say, fumbling to answer it.

Spike stares at me, wide-eyed for a moment, then gathers up the takeaway containers, making far too much noise as he rinses them in the sink and hurls them into the bin.

'Shit. Sorry about that,' I say as I hang up and put my phone on silent. 'It was just Taylor checking about practice. I don't know why I answered. What were you saying?'

'Nothing, Paige. The moment is well and truly over.' Spike's looking busy in the kitchen, while I sit at the dining table watching him, trying to reconnect. He doesn't look up.

'Seriously, I want to know. You were talking about

talking to Lou, about us all being friends?'

'I was talking about talking to her about us, Paige. You and me. But forget it. How are you going to get your Victrola home? Uber?'

'Oh, no, I've got my bike. Can I pick it up another time? I love it – did I already say that?'

Spike smiles half-heartedly. 'You did. I'm glad. I'll catch you soon, okay?' And then he kicks me out into the cold night.

seventeen

'**O**h my god, I've got it!'

We've just finished rehearsing some of Lou's songs. We sound pretty good – simple chords beneath poppy lyrics sung in Lou's sweet, strong voice. Lex looks like he could play the drum parts in his sleep though. Or maybe he's just mulling over what he says next.

'Lou Key and the ... wait for it ...' He does a drum roll.

We look at him eagerly.

'Lunacy! Lou Key and the Lunacy. Brilliant. That's our name. Done.' He does a classic punchline *ba-doom-cha!* on his kit and we all applaud.

'That is pretty good,' I say.

'Pretty good?' Lex feigns horror at the adjective. 'Dude, it's brilliant.'

'How about Lou Key and the Lunatics?' I suggest. 'It kind of makes more sense.'

'Or Lou Key and the Lunar-kicks?'

'What? No, that's awful,' Lex exasperates as Spike and I start brainstorming again.

'Lou Key and the Lunatic Kicks. Lou Key and the Lunar Three – ooh, that's quite cool.'

'Why are we lunatics? I don't get it.'

'Well, you're not, Lou, just the three of us. You're Lou Key.'

She rolls her eyes.

'Yeah, but our name is Lou Key and the Lunacy,' Lex says, pouting. 'I was really proud when I came up with that.'

'Aw, Lex. It's really good.' Spike gives him a thumbs-up.

Lex pouts further before conceding, 'Actually, Lou Key and the Lunar Three is pretty ace.'

'Yeah, I like that too. Lunar over lunacy. Much more serious,' I add. We look at Lou.

'I like it too,' she says. 'Nice one, Spike. Should we try it out for a bit? See if it sticks?'

I try to catch Spike's eye, but he won't look at me. I haven't seen his face all practice. I'm still hoping for a smile when Lex counts us in and we start to run through our set again with the renewed sense of importance and unification that comes from having a name.

The simplicity of Lou's songs work and she's a good singer, so the backup doesn't need to be too complex or distracting. Her lyrics are straightforward and I've felt more inspired than ever to get my own songwriting going.

I've borrowed an acoustic guitar and I've been quietly working on material in my room most days. The trip home really lent itself to being lyricised and I've been thinking a lot about forgiveness. Dylan's 'Don't Think Twice, it's All Right' keeps coming to mind. The more I think about it, it's actually kind of bitter. It's a song about moving on and getting used to having to move on because people keep letting you down; the idea that your time has been wasted with someone, but they shouldn't waste their own time feeling bad about that. It's an excellent song, but I think I want to write something a bit more compassionate. Mum left us years ago and when she finally came back, I was the one to leave. But I don't think you can ever truly leave someone while you're still alive. I went back and left again and at some stage she's probably going to leave us forever. It's not all right in the dismissive way Dylan means it, but it is kind of – somehow – okay.

I play through my latest song on the topic:

You're not the only reason I moved on
to a place that knows my lines
you're not the only reason I moved on
moving on was just a matter of time
here the tree-lined streets turn golden with age
and I feel the change of rhythm filling my page
leaving gives the wind a chance to blow through my hair
and sorrow gives my friends a chance to show that they care
and now we're both years older
I can stop wishing you were always there for me.

I find myself understanding more and more why Mum might have felt the urge to be somewhere else. I mean, she left her family behind, which is huge, but I'm starting to understand the drive to leave a place. Dylan's the master of moving on, of course. Maybe it's something you just get used to.

*

I haven't eaten all day and have a rehearsal with Virginia's Wolf this afternoon. I don't have to check the kitchen to know what's there. I can only afford to buy food on an as-needed basis and I haven't been to the supermarket in weeks.

I'm running out the front door when something on the porch catches my eye. A bright red suitcase with a crushed bow on it and a record-sized plastic bag.

Spike dropped off my present.

I take it inside and grab my bike, wondering if it was placed there out of generosity or as an extension of kicking me out. I remember breathing him in as I hugged him. I should call him.

As I park my bike and lock it to the railing, I hear a busker outside the shopping centre. He's playing The Smiths, 'There is a Light That Never Goes Out' – one of the darkest and yet most optimistic songs ever. I walk closer and realise that not only are the lyrics familiar, but the voice is too. It's Taylor.

I give him a look of astonished joy and mouth the words to the chorus with him. He grins and winks at me, singing a little louder until the song's fade out. I give him a round of applause and he calls me over.

'Thanks. I think I've even made a bit of coin today. What are you up to?'

'I'm on my way to rehearsal but needed some food first. Are you taking a break?'

'I'd love to. I'll pack up and come with you.' Taylor's already scraping the coins out of his guitar case. I bend down to give him a hand.

'I didn't know you busked,' I say.

'I just come out when I feel like it, really. It's a chance to play a few covers and try out some new stuff. I like the fact that no one's really listening. It's liberating.'

I laugh. 'I was listening. Heard your Morrissey impression from way down the street. Great song choice.'

'I'm glad you like it. It's so miserably optimistic. Not a good one to sing on a road trip though,' he says, zipping up his case. 'What do you feel like eating?'

We end up at an outside table and I spend the last of my loose change on a bowl of noodles. Taylor orders the same. It's jacket and hat weather and the food warms me from the inside.

'I've never busked,' I confess between mouthfuls.

'You should! Or we could. Or, you know, you could,' Taylor says.

'I think I'd like to. I've been writing a bunch of songs on the acoustic. I'm no good really, but I could set myself a challenge – to be good enough to be ignored by the shoppers at Barkly Square.'

'A fine goal!' Taylor chuckles. 'I recommend it. And you don't have to be that great. It's been a confidence booster for playing my solo stuff. I'm thinking of doing a bit more with my own material actually.'

A pang of panic hits me. 'What about Agent Smith?'

'Oh, I still need Agent Smith. I think we should be looking at recording and touring, actually. There's a festival coming up I want to book us for.'

'I've never been to a festival!' I blurt, like a kid who's been told they're going to Disneyland.

'Well, this could be your chance!'

'Actually, Virginia's Wolf mentioned something about a festival too. We haven't played anywhere yet though, so Maree's worried it's not the best first gig for us. I don't care though. I'd just love to be part of something big like that.'

'Mate, you could play with us. Get Virginia's Wolf and your other band with Lou on board ... plus your solo stuff ... Actually, on second thoughts, let's organise a separate festival just in your honour. All Paige, all the time. I'm there,' Taylor mocks.

'Well, you'd have to be there because Agent Smith,' I say, deadpan.

'Oh. True.' Taylor slurps up his noodles decisively. 'But seriously. It would be a good gig and if you're going to be there anyway, I reckon you should book in a little solo show. Why the hell not?'

'Because I've never played solo before!' A couple at the

next table look over. I lower my voice and eyeball Taylor. 'I'm not ready.'

'But you could be. Okay, here's your challenge. Practise in your room for a bit. Then come here and play for the indifferent shoppers. Then play your first gig at this festival. I think you have ...' Taylor counts up the months on his fingers. It doesn't take long. 'Three months!'

'Oh my god,' I groan, but there's a twinkle of excitement too.

'Or ...' Taylor gets a wily look in his eye. 'You could take my guitar now and just go for it! Deep end!' He holds his guitar out for me and nods towards his busking spot.

I laugh. 'If those are the options, I'll go for the first.'

'Excellent! I love that option because it ends with you playing a solo set at the festival in three months.'

'I liked it because it starts with me playing solo in my room.'

'I know,' says Taylor, patting me on the arm. 'I know.'

*

After lunch, I bike on to Virginia's Wolf rehearsal. We set up in Maree's living room and struggle through the first two songs. It's not coming easily. The double bass I'm borrowing has to stay here, since I don't have any means of transporting it, so I haven't practised my parts. This has always been my problem with the double bass. And to be honest, I've mostly been focussing on acoustic guitar and playing my own songs in my spare time.

We have to stop and restart this rehearsal several times.

'Gah!' An exasperated cry from Becca. 'I'm not sure we're really gelling, you know?'

We all look at her as she throws up her arms.

'It's not sounding great,' Charlie agrees.

Is it my fault? I should be taking this band much more

seriously, but it's hard when Agent Smith is booked up and busy and Lou's band are my best friends. I guess I've been prioritising elsewhere.

'Sorry,' I say. 'I haven't had a chance to learn my parts.' There's no point pretending I know what I'm doing.

'It's not your fault, but I really want to book us a show soon. How are people feeling about that?' Maree asks.

'A show? I think that's a great idea, but we're far from ready. I mean, we're far from being close to even thinking about being ready,' Becca says.

Maree's face drops.

'I'd love us to play a show, but we need to do way better than this.' Tess writes the songs and knows her guitar parts perfectly. When she says 'we' she means the rest of us.

As we each put our instruments down and take a seat, I think this is the most demoralising band practice I've ever been at. I'm used to things going wrong in much more dramatic ways – band mates storming out shouting abuse. Here we're all just quietly reflecting on how much we suck. It's grim.

After a while I add my two cents, 'Maybe a goal like a booked show is what we need to really motivate us. Maybe this is hard because we're not focussed on an outcome.' It sounds like something Taylor would say – band manager speak.

No one says anything. I wish I hadn't either.

Group silence makes me uncomfortable, but when I'm about to say something else, Tess shoots me a look. 'Let's keep this conversation fair. We can each say our part when we're ready to.'

God. This is agonising.

'I'm feeling ... that we need to come together more often with a greater feeling of shared purpose.'

'I'm feeling ... that I really want to get our music out

there, but I'm willing to wait until everyone in the band feels ready.'

I stifle an eye roll. I'm feeling ... impatient and like I need to play some rock and roll. I'm not cut out to be a folk musician.

eighteen

Caz stares as I rush in, throw my bag out back and clumsily tie my apron on.

'I know, I know!' I say, 'I'm so so so sorry.'

She shakes her head. 'Lucky for you we have been coping admirably without you, but Rob is not happy. He hates lateness.'

'Yeah, he told me. I can't promise it will never happen again, but I would like to point out that it has never happened before,' I say, shuffling dockets around and trying to look useful.

'Latte and a flat white.' Caz nudges two coffees towards me. 'Table eight.'

I take them, feeling ashamed. It really is unlike me to be late, but I guess pointing that out doesn't help the fact that there was work to do and I wasn't here to do it. I wish it wasn't my fault too. I wish I could say the tram broke down, or there was an emergency, or I got a flat tyre, or I was saving children from a burning building, but the truth is I just lost track of time.

The stream of coffees to be delivered keeps coming, and I'm trying to be extra efficient – clearing tables on my way past, checking in with the kitchen – to remind everyone what an exceptional employee I am. I don't know if anyone notices.

As the coffee crowd thins, the tension behind the counter relaxes.

'All right. Tell me about him,' says Caz. It's the first non-work thing she's said to me all day.

'Tell you about who?'

'Well, you were running late this morning with no explanation, you've been hurrying home at the end of your shifts and, most telling of all, you're floating around the place with the most distracted expression I've ever seen. Spill.' She looks expectantly at me. 'And now you're blushing. Nailed it. Tell me everything.'

'Oh no ...' I groan and then laugh. 'There's no one. Seriously, I've just been ...'

'It's Spike, isn't it? I could tell by the way he looked at you last time he came in. Do you *loooooove* him?' she teases. She reminds me of Rose.

'Really, it's nothing like that.' Spike's still mad at me. I don't want to be reminded.

'Whatever. Love is what we're all seeking, right? So, I'm happy for you. Lose yourself in it, totally. Why the hell not?'

'I'm not in love,' I mutter, but Caz hasn't finished.

'Just don't leave me hanging when there are coffees to deliver. I told Rob you texted me you were running late. I lied to the boss for you. Don't make me do that again.' Her tone is teasing, but she has a good point.

'I'm so sorry. I'll be better.'

'I'm sure you will be. But Rob wants a word with you, regardless.'

*

Rob gave me a verbal warning, meaning if I don't sort my shit out pronto, I risk losing the one thing that's (only just) keeping me off the streets. Thank god for Agent Smith.

Our last Virginia's Wolf practice left me feeling more than a little uninspired. Their lack of enthusiasm and confidence makes me wonder if we'll ever graduate from living room to stage. And now Lou Key and the Lunar Three are arguing over something I've lost track of. All this drama makes me want to go solo – retreat into my own singer-songwriter angst.

Lou's not happy. That much I have gathered.

Lex is trying to cheer her up. 'It's going to be fine! Fun even,' he says.

'I just don't think these songs work with a band. They're solos. They always have been. I don't know what I was thinking.'

'Woah,' I tune in. 'You don't like what we're doing here? I thought it sounded really good. In my humble opinion.'

'I just think it's a bit of a weird dynamic – you know, a band made up of,' she gestures vaguely at us, '"friends".' You can hear the air quotes in her voice. 'With all our, you know, history.'

'I think you're overthinking it,' I say. 'And what do you mean history? We're all good.'

Spike shoots me an inscrutable look.

'Maybe we need some feedback,' I suggest.

Lou sighs.

'What's wrong with that? It's a good suggestion,' Lex says.

'I'm just starting to think I liked it better solo.'

'Lou, are you breaking up with us?' I say, dramatically lifting my bass off my body and miming throwing it on the floor. 'Because I don't know if I can handle that right now!'

'Oh my god.' Apparently Spike can't handle any of this.

'I'm serious, Paige. Everything is always such a joke to

you.' Lou's glaring at me. She probably really means it, but it makes me laugh. 'See! You're laughing right now. This is really important to me!'

'Lou, come on. It's a bit out of the blue, isn't it? What's up with you?' Spike asks, raising his hands in a gesture of peace and defeat.

It seems to work ... sort of. Lou bursts into tears. She sobs herself off to Lex's room, so Spike and I decide to abandon the practice. When she's ready, she'll call another one.

Spike's looked me in the eye twice now and has even lowered himself to slowly biking with me towards the bike path.

'She's a bit emotional sometimes. I don't know why. I've known her a while and haven't figured out all her triggers.'

'She's so up and down. It makes her hard to be around,' I say.

'Sure, but how must it be for her?'

'Was I a bit of a jerk back there? You and Lex know Lou better than I do. I should have tiptoed, but I didn't know I was supposed to. I totally said the wrong thing.'

Spike makes a kind of scoffing noise.

'What?'

'Gee, Paige, what do you think?' His sarcasm burns. Third-degree. His face is all hard lines.

I can't deal, and it's probably the least mature thing I've ever done, but I pick up the pace and ride clumsily away without another word.

*

'How's the solo career coming, Paige?' It appears Taylor hasn't forgotten my challenge.

'It's becoming more and more appealing as my other

projects fray at the edges,' I answer, clipping my bass into its case. We're packing up after an Agent Smith practice.

'Oh?' Taylor looks surprised.

'Well, not this project, obviously. This is going swimmingly. I guess I'm realising that I like having a bit more control over things. Musically, I mean.'

'Oh, definitely! I wouldn't cope without my solo projects. Musically, I mean,' Taylor says. 'Are you still writing? Nearly ready for your Barkly Square debut?'

'I'm getting there. I've been practising heaps and some of my songs are bordering on passable. Performing them in front of people, however, will be a different story.'

'I can't wait! Maybe you could try them in front of a small friendly audience first. Play at a party or something.'

'That's not a bad idea.' It reminds me of my perfectly reasonable suggestion that we get some feedback for Lou's band. And my other very reasonable suggestion that Virginia's Wolf set a performance goal to work towards.

'We could organise a party for that very purpose if you'd like.'

'Why are you so dedicated to this cause?' I ask.

'It's a noble cause! And I liked what you played for me that time in my lounge. You have solo potential written all over you.'

'I do, eh? And ... you want to be my manager and take a fifty per cent cut. I'm onto you.' I eye Taylor suspiciously.

'Caught me. I'm all about the profit.' He laughs. 'Catch you next time.' He picks up his guitar case and disappears out of the band room before I can say anything else.

*

'It sounds a bit like you have a problem playing music with other women.' Lily's face fills my screen. She has a new haircut and looks super hip.

'What? No I don't!'

'But it's just Lou and Virginia Woolf that you're struggling to play with?'

'Virginia's Wolf. And I'm not struggling, they are. All they do is sit around and talk about feelings and be-careful-what-you-say. It's not as rock and roll as I'm used to.' Actually, maybe she's right. It does sound bad.

'Maybe the world needs a bit *more* sitting around and talking about feelings. Maybe people *should* be careful what they say.' Lily's in full swing. 'I'm not getting at you, Paige, I know you're a feminist, but I think you might need to reflect a bit on this. You've always got on well with the guys in your bands. Can't you see the women as allies too? Why should they have to shout and rock out and act like guys to gain your respect?'

I think of my reaction to Lou, to Spike. I can't even begin to defend myself. 'Goddamn it. Fine. You might be right. Okay, Lily, maybe music should be about feelings and care and compassionate conversations too. Maybe there's room for all of it.'

'And you are all of those things *and* a completely crazy rock chick! Embrace it all!'

I laugh. 'That's a wonderfully confusing message. Thank you.'

'You're welcome. Hey, when can we come and visit you? Soon?'

'Any time! Please come.'

'Okay. We'll start saving.' She grins a grin I've known for years.

'Hopefully there'll be a gig you can come to. Maybe a bunch of them.'

'I can't wait. I miss you.'

'I miss you too!'

Lily's right. Actually, everybody's right. I do need to be more open to different styles of music and different bands' ways of operating. I need to listen better to Lou. I need to keep practising my parts in my own time so I can contribute to a better sound. I need to book myself a house party gig and play some of my solo stuff to an audience. I need to take control. Taylor's place would be the best for a party and I reckon I can get all my bands to play something – it will be the push they all need. I don't suppose we even need an occasion to celebrate, but it would be nice to have one. I get out my notebook and start making lists. It will be like organising a mini festival. A dress rehearsal before the real event in a few months' time.

I start with a message to Taylor to secure the venue. Three weeks should be enough time to get ready. Then I send a group message to The Lunar Three and another to Virginia's Wolf, making sure I sound enthusiastic yet business-like. People respect that. I don't want to sound like I'm asking and giving them a chance to opt out. I strongly feel that we should all do this.

Taylor replies. *Ah the Paige Festival! It's happening! Absolutely we can book that in. Should we pretend it's your birthday or something?*

I look over my solo songs – I have about five I would be willing to play to an audience. I can practise those and put the writing on hold for a bit while I try to get better at guitar. Sometimes I can hear the song in my head but I'm not good enough to recreate the sound as I imagined it. I really want to be in control of this. Control. It's becoming quite the theme.

nineteen

'Bridge Over Troubled Water' is blaring out of Lou's room. She's been playing Simon and Garfunkel all day and I have reached my absolute limit.

I storm through her door.

She's sitting cross-legged on her bed with her eyes closed and the most blissed-out expression on her face. Is she meditating? With this racket going on? She seems to sense my presence and holds up a hand to silence my not-yet-uttered protest. Then, as if conducting me, she moves her hand in a welcoming gesture, drawing me into the room and pointing to the seat next to her. There's half a beat's pause in the song and then the next verse starts, the crescendo rising again. There's no use trying to speak, so I sit and close my eyes with Lou, let the song fill me. God, I hate Simon and Garfunkel.

Eventually the music fades, and Lou reaches over and gives me a hug. 'Thank you,' she says.

'What for?'

'That was beautiful. Thank you for sharing it with me.'

'Oh, well, I was actually coming in to ask you to turn it down. But, yeah, that was all right.'

'My parents used to listen to Simon and Garfunkel in the car when we went on family road trips. We always sang along loudest to "I am a Rock" and "America". I love them.'

'My parents used to listen to them too, but I am not a fan,' I say.

Lou ignores me, 'Oh and once when I was really angry with my mum about something, I remember her quoting bits of "Bridge Over Troubled Water" to me, reminding me she was on my side. I was kind of angry in high school.'

I refrain from adding my two cents.

'The songwriting is top-notch, don't you think? And their voices – totally angelic harmonies!' She looks at me. 'What on earth don't you like about them?'

'I just find it so ... ordinary. Where's the grit? The struggle? Where's the protest that typifies that era of folk music?'

'Are you kidding me?' Lou's bounced out of her meditative pose and is looming over me. She sounds mad. 'They were a hundred per cent in the thick of the counterculture of the protest movement, leading the social revolution alongside The Beatles and Bob Dylan.'

'What did they have to revolt against? They grew up in New York, never had to leave town to get famous, to make their way on their own. You can hear the privilege in their choir boy voices and soppy poppy songs.'

Lou's mouth is wide in disbelief. She looks like she could mortally wound me with that look. I should probably go.

'Anyway,' I continue. 'Dylan hated them.'

'No, he didn't!' she shouts. 'They had very similar careers, actually! They were even signed to the same label.'

I didn't actually know that.

'And why the hell would you hate something just because Bob Dylan hated it? He's the most cynical old curmudgeon the music scene has ever known!'

I'm standing in the doorway now. Fuming.

Lou's eyes are wide. She seems to recoil, physically.

Then she starts giggling. 'Oh my god. I'm so sorry.' She's gasping and looking at me as if I've morphed into something comical.

I feel like I've been slapped.

She pats the space on the bed where I was sitting. 'Sorry, I'm sorry, Paige. Sit down. Let me play something for you.'

Reluctantly, I sit down again. I have nothing better to do today than argue about folk music. Plus, aren't I trying to be more open?

Lou flips through some CDs and puts one in her chunky old Sony stereo.

'I love that you have a CD collection,' I tell her, my voice calming.

'I love CDs. They're so old school. Listen to this.' She hits play and something familiar, yet strange and synthy starts playing.

'What is this? Is that an accordion?' Drums burst out like controlled explosions.

'This is "The Boy in the Bubble", from Paul Simon's *Graceland*. This is his best solo album.'

His choir boy voice has changed into something stronger, and there's a sense of urgency and an optimism in the rising major shifts.

'After he split with Art Garfunkel, his career was dwindling and he got very depressed, but then he had a stroke of genius in the mid-80s and wrote this album in South Africa. It's my number one top favourite album of all time,' Lou says.

I raise my eyebrows at her. 'Really?'

'Mm-hm. Listen.' She closes her eyes and puts her hand on top of mine.

I stifle a laugh, but it's not a laughing-at-her laugh. It's a laugh of surprised pleasure. I close my eyes too.

Musically, *Graceland* is incredible. It soars in and out of pop and improvisation, layers of melody weaving through each song. There's African beats and rhythm. The lyrics are sometimes hilarious and conversational and other times poetic and an astute commentary on modern culture. Sometimes it seems to be both major and minor at the same time. We listen to the whole thing. Lou tells me about all the times she's come back to this album in her life, listening to it with her mum, playing it for boyfriends who pretended to know the lyrics. In 'Call Me Al' there's an epic fretless bass solo, that Lou tells me was pre-recorded and added to the song backwards in post-production.

'This is what music's supposed to do,' Lou declares.

I think I know what she means.

When the album finishes, I go and get my shiny red Victrola and records, while Lou runs downstairs and grabs a bottle of red wine from the kitchen. We take turns playing each other our favourite tracks, vinyl to CD and back, explaining the significance of each. Turns out we have a lot in common. Time darkens the windows in Lou's room, but we're warm, lit, singing along.

I tell her about each of the records Spike gave me, what the songs mean to me, what I learnt about life while listening to them; also, the way Spike's knowledge and enthusiasm always helped me love something new.

'You love him, don't you?' Lou asks.

I'm quiet for a moment. 'He's important to me, yeah,' is all I can let her have.

I pull out *Blue*. 'Now this is one I'm still learning to love,' I say as I slide the vinyl out of the sleeve and place it gently on the turntable. 'Last year when my mum came to visit, she gave me this album. It's her favourite. Dad must have said something about me liking records, but I was surprised she liked something so folky. She says it's poetry.'

I set the needle down and 'All I Want' jangles out with the determined, sweet, melancholic first chords. Lou closes her eyes and smiles through the intro. I can't help but smile too. She looks so ... *involved*. We both start singing as Joni does, but I lose the lyrics quickly.

'God, how great is Joni Mitchell?' Lou says. 'I mean, imagine what it would have taken to hold your own as a woman in that era of privileged white male egos. No offence to your beloved Dylan.' She laughs at my mock filthy look. 'I mean, I know you love his music and I get that. He stood for things and cared about the world and that's totally important. But Joni ... she makes herself so vulnerable. Just being a woman, falling in love, finding yourself ... that's totally – what did you call it? Grit and struggle? It's all there just in being alive. Being open to getting your heart broken.'

'Stay romantic,' I mumble. I trace my finger around the bright edge of the Victrola. It really is the nicest thing anyone's ever given me.

Lou's still talking. 'It's scary opening up to people, but imagine refusing to feel the things she's singing about?' I don't know if she's still talking about Joni Mitchell. I don't know if she's incredibly drunk or incredibly wise, but suddenly the music is getting to me and my tears are real.

'Oh, Paige!' Lou gives me a hug.

I shake my head. 'It's fine.' I wipe my sleeve over my eyes. 'I'm fine. Like I said, I'm still learning to love this one.'

'You will. This album's a classic.'

'I didn't know you knew so much about music, Lou.' She gives me a funny look.

'I mean I know you're a musician, duh, I just mean, you care so much about the stories, you've read the interviews, watched the docos ... I don't know many people like that.' I think back to the Vox Pop days, with Spike and Ed always discussing music at a level I was desperate to reach.

'Music's the only thing I really care about, you know?' She gets that same blissed-out expression on her face as she had when I first came in to ask her to turn her shit music down.

'Well, that's the kind of thing I say too, but it's not entirely true. I care about all sorts of things – people, climate change, cat videos.'

She lets out a quick laugh, then looks at me intensely. 'I mean it though. I couldn't keep going without music.'

I believe her.

twenty

Virginia's Wolf have cancelled all practices until further notice and my party plans are going terribly.

'I can't organise a party just so I can debut my solo stuff! How narcissistic is that?' I'm despairing to Caz between coffee orders.

'You really can't,' she says. 'It's weird.'

'What do I do? Lou only wants to play solo. And everyone else is far from enthused.' I'm waving my arms about like a lunatic.

'I think I'm just telling you what you already know, but you can only have complete control when you're solo. Collaborating means being more flexible. So leave the gig-booking to the band managers.'

I'm inconsolable. And table eight needs clearing.

After my shift, I have a missed call from a random number. I call it back and find I'm being asked to play an Alanis Morissette tribute show. The organisers want me to choose one song from the *Jagged Little Pill* album and play it in two weeks' time. I have no idea who put my name forward (actually I have a strong suspicion Taylor put my name forward). I should call him.

Honestly, I haven't listened to a whole lot of Alanis Morissette. I know the singles from that album – who doesn't? – but it came out five years before I was born. Still,

Blood on the Tracks came out twenty-five years before I was born, and I know every single note and lyric on that album. Anyway, I agreed to do it and am now listening intently to the album. It's pretty good. Only a few songs would really work solo though.

I'm sitting on my bed, with my laptop. I'm not 100% ready to give up my mini-festival idea, but it is a little spooky how the Alanis Morissette gig came up just as I was feeling at a loss. Maybe that's the optimist's job: to point out when things seem to be falling perfectly into place and to quietly endure the times when they don't. (Caz and Spike might disagree about the 'quietly' aspect of my endurance.)

My phone's on silent, but I see a call come through. I answer before turning the music down. It's Maree.

'Is that Alanis in the background?' she asks. 'Angsty. You okay?'

'Hey, Maree. Yeah, I'm fine. Just listening to *Jagged Little Pill*. I've been asked to play one of the tracks at a tribute show.'

'That's so cool. I love Alanis. From that album, I would say "All I Really Want" is my fav track. It's hard to choose though, right? You should check out the *Jagged Little Pill* tour on YouTube. She was such a rock star.'

Huh. I hadn't picked Maree for a rock fan. 'I'll definitely look for that. Thanks.' I'm searching for it as we speak.

'Oh man, 1995 was a truly excellent year for music.'

'I know, right? Sometimes I wish I was born twenty years earlier.'

'Me too! But then, of course, we'd be pushing forty now and quite frankly, screw that!'

'Oh god.' That doesn't bear thinking about.

'And, actually our generation – I mean we missed some pretty ace bands at the peak of their brilliance – but our generation has so many more opportunities. Musically, I mean.'

I chuckle at this. She sounds like me. 'Totally. So ... what's up?'

'Oh right! I didn't call to talk about grunge and the 90s and being forty.' She sounds so animated. 'I wanted to tell you that we've changed our minds about the party. Of course we'll play it. It would be cool and thank you for organising it. I think you're right. It will focus some of our next practices too. And hey, it will give us all a better sense of how we're feeling about the band. Whether we should keep going.'

I decide to shelve the implications of that last comment for a later date. This is great news. 'Yay! I'm so glad! I just need to convince the other bands. At this point, it looks like we'll have solo sets from me and Lou and then band-wise we've got Agent Smith and now ... yay ... Virginia's Wolf!'

'A formidable line-up. We'd be honoured,' Maree declares.

'Excellent.'

'I'm going to go listen to Alanis too.'

'Awesome. Do it. Catch you later.'

'I'll text you tomorrow about our next practice.'

'Okay.' I hang up first. I'm so excited, I send a message to Spike.

He calls me instantly. 'So ... wow. You're organising a party and playing solo at an Alanis tribute gig! You rock!' I can picture his wide grin.

'I'm so excited! And you know, maybe it's okay if Lou plays solo. I've got two other bands.'

'Yeah, it is okay, but that kind of defeats the point of letting the band play to an audience. Getting a second opinion and all that.'

'Oh yeah. That was the point, eh? Do you think ... I

mean ... You want to play, right? Could you talk to Lou? Try and convince her it's a good idea?'

'I can try. I mean it *is* a good idea.' Spike seems to be choosing his words carefully. 'And of course I want to play – I'm not a rock star like you with five thousand different projects on the go. The Lunar Three is pretty much it for me. I need all the gigs I can get.'

'Awww.'

'Yeah, poor me, right?' Spike laughs. 'I'll talk to Lou. Now, tell me more about Alanis. Who's organising it? How did they find you?'

'It's being organised by someone called Lane ... or Blaine or something. I don't know. I'm pretty sure Taylor put my name down for it. He's been angling for me to play a solo gig for ages.'

There's an odd silence on the other end. I let it sit. 'I see.' Spike's enthusiasm has dropped several notches. He sounds almost disinterested.

'Are you okay?' I ask.

'Yeah, I'm good!' And now he's a little too perky. What have I done now? 'Hey, I'd better go. I'll talk to Lou about the party. It's at Taylor's, right?'

'Yeah, in two weeks – the night before the tribute show. Yikes! Anyway, Taylor's place is great for parties. And it was something Taylor said that helped me come up with the idea. Or maybe it was Taylor's idea. Anyway ...' I'm suddenly aware of the silence at the other end again and the fact that I've said Taylor's name about a thousand times.

'Right. Well. I'd better go.' Spike's gone cold on me, again.

My stomach does that elevator thing where it kind of falls suddenly. 'Okay. Well, I hope you're okay and thanks for calling. Thanks for being excited for me,' I say. My words seem to hang in the space between us.

'No problem. Later.' He hangs up first.

The shine of my recent news has dulled, but I turn up Alanis. She gets it.

*

It's quiet in the house as usual, but the neighbour's gate is squeaking in the wind. A squeak and then a clatter as it doesn't quite latch itself closed. Over and over.

I can't get to sleep. My brain is busy with all the things I need to organise for this party – equipment, people etc. I know Taylor will help me and Greg will have gear to borrow if we need it, but I feel really bad about the end of that phone call with Spike. Am I doing something wrong with Taylor? Have Spike and Taylor talked about me? Does Spike know something I don't? My mind sticks on this for a while then flits inevitably to the part where I've been shoving my real worries.

I'm rostered on tomorrow. My only shift this week – Rob's mad at me. I have no idea how I'm going to survive here if I don't make some money soon.

Squeak and a clatter. Over and over.

I'm almost ready to run out there in my pyjamas and latch the gate shut myself.

*

I bump into Shaun outside Vinyl.

'Long time, Paige! What's been happening?'

'Hey!' The months have flown by. 'I've been playing a bunch of gigs with Agent Smith, practising with other bands. I've been writing my own stuff too.'

'Nice. Sounds excellent, yeah? How's everything going at home?'

'Oh, no change with Mum. Thanks for asking. She's starting another round of treatment.' How do I change the subject? 'I mean, she's still sick ...' I actually haven't thought about Mum stuff for ages.

Shaun puts his hand on my shoulder and nods slowly.

'Hey, I'm organising a party – you guys have to come!' My change of subject is jarring. Even to me.

'Sounds cool, yeah? What's the occasion?' Shaun asks.

'Well, it's a chance for some of the projects I'm involved in to play to an audience. I thought it would be a nice, non-threatening way to start.'

'You having trouble booking gigs?'

'No, it's not that. We're just in the early stages and not quite ready to charge strangers to listen to us!' I laugh.

'It sounds cool, yeah? Any way I can help out? Or Nic Cage and the Bad Leads? Or Ghostwriters? Or, you know, I'm playing with Goldlust more now, yeah? Maybe they could get in on it? They have a pretty epic following.'

'I hadn't even thought of asking other bands. I was selfishly fixated on playing bass with as many different bands as possible on the same night!' I joke. This event could blow up.

'Wicked personal challenge, yeah?' Shaun nods.

'This could turn into something huge! In a good way. I'll figure some things out and let you know.' This could be my John Lee Hooker moment. It only took one gig for Dylan to get his big break in New York. Maybe there'll be a scout or someone famous who recognises something in me and takes me under their wing.

Shaun's looking at me funny. I snap back to the present.

'Cool – well, I'm sure we can make it work if you'd like us to, yeah? I'd better run. So good to bump into you, Paige. Be in touch, yeah?'

'For sure. I'd better get in there and start my shift. Good to see you, Shaun.'

I rush into Vinyl and grab my apron from out the back. Another shift on minimum sleep. At least I'm getting better at this.

*

Taylor turns up at the busiest time of the day.

'Hey!' I call as I rush past with an armful of dishes.

He's paying for a takeaway coffee and calling across the café to me. 'Hey, man, you look busy. When do you finish? I'll come back. We need to talk.'

'Sounds ominous,' I say. 'We close at five. Come back then?'

'I will! Not ominous. Business stuff. Catch you later.' He waits around for his takeaway coffee then strolls out the door.

My head is swimming with table numbers, coffee orders, band names and things I need to do when I finish here.

But when the end of my shift draws near, it's Spike, not Taylor, who's waiting at the café door.

'Hey. Can we talk after your shift? Walk you home?' he says.

'Oh. Yeah, sure. Umm, I have my bike.'

'Well, can we sit in the park for a bit when you're done, then?'

'Okay,' I smile at him as I retie my apron and lift a chair onto a table. 'I still have to clean up, but I've been wanting to call you. I've been thinking a lot, listening to Joni Mitchell and all that stuff about vulnerability.' I'm rambling. 'Anyway. You okay?'

Spike almost-smiles. 'Look, I understand that—'

'I'm late but I'm here! Let's talk business!' Taylor walks in already talking. I hate when people do that.

Spike's face drops. Truly terrible timing.

'Hi, Taylor. I'm nearly done here, but Spike's waiting for me.'

'I just need five minutes. It's about Paigefest.'

'What the fuck is Paigefest?' Spike asks, scowling at Taylor.

'It's what Taylor calls this party we're organising. Actually, I had some ideas too,' I say to Taylor. Shaun's suggestion has grown in my imagination over the last few hours.

'So, are you guys having a meeting or something? Did you want to talk to me or not, Paige?' Spike's voice is getting louder.

'I do want to talk to you,' I say. 'I just—'

Taylor interrupts again, 'I said I would be back at the end of your shift, Paige. Five minutes?'

Caz calls out to me to finish the clean-up. Spike looks hurt.

'Guys, I'm still working. Give me a few minutes to finish.' I rush out the back and grab the mop, leaving Taylor and Spike to size each other up.

Paigefest indeed.

In the end, Taylor tells me the problem, leaning in the doorway while I mop the floor. (Spike left before I could stop him.) We can't hold the party at Taylor's. There are housemates and neighbours and noise concerns. I thought he'd sorted all that. Did this only just occur to him? I don't know whether to just give up or bite the bullet and go bigger.

*

At home, sitting at the dining table, I ask Lou for advice.

'Lou, do you think this party is a good idea? My venue fell through and I don't know if I should try and find somewhere else or just chuck in the whole project.'

She comes to sit beside me. 'I think it could be huge!' Her eyes are wider than usual. 'What if we could find a warehouse or something and invite a heap more bands to play. I'll give you some of my contacts. We could make it epic!' She's gesturing emphatically and nearly hits me in the face.

Her enthusiasm makes me nervous. 'I actually am kind of keen to persevere, just to see if I could make it happen. It could be fun, but I've never organised anything like this before, apart from the odd gig or house party back home.'

'It will be amazing!' Lou cries.

I slip back into that fame reverie I keep having, where that one gig launches my musical career. It almost feels possible, showcasing my talent as a bass player in a surf-rock band, my songwriting with a solo set, and my double bass skills in a folk band. Something's bound to come out of it, especially if we get a good crowd.

'Do you know about any warehouses ...?' I ask.

'I'm bound to know someone who knows someone! You know how these things work,' she says. 'I'll ask around.'

'Thanks,' I say, secretly deciding to do some groundwork on this myself. Just in case. I still haven't got the measure of Lou and her wildly varying moods. 'And I'm going to ask Ghostwriters to play – you think Lex will be keen? – and Shaun's other bands. We could have quite the line-up.' I'm starting to feel excited. This is going to happen.

'I could get my designer friend to help with promo if you like.' Lou's leaning forward, her face a little too close to mine.

'Sure!' At this point, anything would be helpful, and I'll just make sure I'm super organised in case Lou flakes out or disappears again. (I seem to still be a little bitter about the dissolution of The Lunar Three.)

I head upstairs and settle in for a practice. I have my

solo stuff to work on, the Alanis gig, Agent Smith and Virginia's Wolf tunes to practise. I have a lot of work to do.

I'm interrupted almost immediately by the doorbell ringing. Where's Lou gone? I run downstairs to answer.

Spike's standing on the doorstep, looking frowny.

'Hi, you. What's up?'

'Can I come in?' His expression doesn't change and his tone matches his frown. He doesn't look pleased to see me. My stomach feels heavy.

We head back up to my room where my amp is humming away. I switch it off and the space becomes white-noisily still.

'So, what's up?' I say again.

'Paige,' he starts, and looks down at his hands.

'Are you okay?'

'Not really.'

This takes me by surprise. 'Oh ...? I've been meaning to call you. Did I say that? I've been so caught up organising this gig, but I've been thinking about you a lot. Really. A lot.' In fact, since that conversation with Lou about *Blue*, I have been wondering what it would feel like to let myself be more vulnerable, more open. I want to let myself feel all the feels. I want to risk great pain for great love. And I want to risk that with Spike. Or I thought I did. Seeing his expression now, I'm struggling. Right now it sounds like a quick way to get hurt.

'Paige, you've kind of been being a jerk to me recently and I want to know what's going on. Are you into Taylor?'

'What?' This is not what I was expecting.

'You're always going on about how great he is and how supportive of your music and blah blah blah. You keep shutting me down when I try to tell you how I feel. So, please would you just tell me to fuck off, so I can stop embarrassing myself.'

'Well, that's mean!' I snap. 'Taylor's my friend and band mate. I don't think I go on about him.'

'Paige, I don't think you think at all. Most people would be more respectful of other people's feelings.'

'Gee, I love being compared to other people,' I mumble. He looks astonished. Why do I get so sarcastic and nasty when Spike gets serious?

'What is that supposed to mean? You better than everyone else now?' he asks.

He's hovering in a flight-or-fight kind of way. I totally get it. I don't want to be here either.

'I'm sorry. I don't know what I meant by that.' And I really don't. 'But I don't think I've done anything wrong. I moved here not knowing anyone and so I made some friends. I don't need you to tell me who I can and can't be friends with.'

'I see.' A classic line for shutting down a conversation. It means nothing.

'Do you? I honestly don't know why you're so upset.' I swallow back the lump in my throat.

'Look, I've been cutting you slack, because yeah, I get it, things have been hard for you with your mum and moving here and everything. But I've been trying to tell you how I feel, I've been trying to be here for you, and you keep shutting me out. I think I'm done.' He gets up to leave.

'Spike, wait!'

'What?' He pauses.

Here's my chance. 'Just ... please ... don't go.' God, is that all I can come up with?

'Bye, Paige.'

I know this feeling. I've been left again. I've screwed up and somehow, without even realising it, I've pushed someone I love away from me. I let the tears out. I lie face down on my bed and vow never to move again, lest I destroy something else I love.

twenty-one

I've dragged myself to a Virginia's Wolf practice. I'm meant to be playing a gig with Agent Smith straight afterwards and all I feel like doing is hiding in my bedroom.

Spike hasn't replied to any of my messages, but I haven't stopped sending them. I've given it a lot of thought and I can see what he meant about me keeping him at a distance. When I got here, I didn't want to lean on him too much. I didn't want to feel like I'd moved here to be with him. I wanted to do it for myself.

Before he always came back when I pushed him away and I guess I figured he always would. But I don't think he's coming back this time, and the thought that he might never talk to me again makes me feel hollow, like an empty soul travelling down an endless road.

At least the band doesn't sound too terrible. I haven't said anything more about the party, so as far as they're all concerned that's what we're practising for. I hope I can pull something off, but at this point, I don't feel very motivated.

'Tell us again who else is playing at this gig, Paige?' Tess asks.

'Well, us, obviously – yay. Umm, Lou Key probably solo but hopefully with the band. Not that we've practised for ages. Me solo, Agent Smith, Ghostwriters definitely and Goldlust hopefully. Oh, and probably Nic Cage and the Bad

Leads since most of their members are also in Ghostwriters.' I hear myself struggling to articulate this list. I can barely string a sentence together.

'Are you okay?'

'What do you mean?'

'Paige, I thought you'd be excited! That's an amazing line-up. It should be so cool!'

'But do you think we even fit with those bands? We're not exactly the same sound,' Charlie says. I've hardly noticed her this practice.

'The solo stuff is kind of folky,' I say, trying (and failing) to muster some enthusiasm.

'It'll be great! I'm sure Paige has it all under control. Okay, let's go from the top again.' Maree gets us back on track and I sit straighter on my stool.

*

The Agent Smith gig is fine. Our set is pretty tight, but it kind of feels like time to add something new. Tonight I feel like I'm going through the motions, struggling to summon my usual energy. The crowd seem to like our set, though.

We ended up playing last in the line-up, and afterwards instead of going out and being part of the crowd as I normally would, I just kind of crashed out in the green room, on a couch upstairs in the dark.

When I get home, the house is uncomfortably quiet. I head upstairs to write in my notebook, feeling more vulnerable than I ever have in my life.

*

I'm on the brink of pulling out of the Alanis tribute show when I turn up to work and *Jagged Little Pill* is playing.

'Who put this on?' I ask before I even greet anyone.

'It's on random,' Caz winks at me.

'No, it's not. And this would never be on a Vinyl playlist anyway. It's nowhere near Triple J enough for us.' It has cheered me up a bit though. Caz starts singing along to the chorus of 'You Learn' rather melodramatically. I laugh and join in.

'This is the song you should do for the tribute show,' she says.

'Did I tell you about that?' The last few days have been a blur of saying things I shouldn't have and not saying things I really should.

Caz looks affronted. 'Who exactly did you think put your name forward?'

'Wait, it was you?! Actually, I thought it was ... Uh, thank you.' I smile at her.

'You're welcome. I thought of you straight away. I'd been trying to put my finger on who you remind me of with your long dark hair and 90s clothes. Alanis was short too.' She gives my hair an affectionate, forceful tousle.

'Ow! I'm glad it was you who set this up for me. I won't let you down!' I give her a salute.

'You'd better not.' She winks again then goes back to work.

I have just over a week to prepare, which is not nearly enough time. But I'm determined. 'Paigefest' is a week away too and I don't know where to start with that. I don't even have a venue. But I've talked it up so much and invited so many musicians to perform ...

'Caz, do you know anyone who has a warehouse?'

'No,' she says, banging the milk jug on the bench. 'Weird question. Why?'

'I need a venue for this party gig event thing I'm supposedly organising for next week.'

'Right. Honestly though, Paige, don't have it in a

warehouse. That's a terrible idea.'

'Oh god, is it?' I'm way out of my depth. Small town wannabe moves to Melbourne to organise a party much cooler than herself. I'm so lame.

'We used to have bands perform here in the courtyard sometimes. Ask Rob. He might be keen to do that again. We could set up a stage in the corner, some fairy lights – you like that sort of thing, right?' she teases.

'Wait. Seriously?'

'Why not? It's a good spot. If Rob okays it, we could close the café and let people in through the back, so it would be exclusive. We've got no neighbours here to complain about the noise.'

'Caz, you are a genius.'

'Yep.' Caz grins. 'Ask Rob first though, eh?'

'I'm not exactly Rob's favourite person at the moment.'

'This could be your chance to redeem yourself.'

'Okay, I'll talk to him. Thank you! Again!' Caz has quietly improved my situation without moving from behind the coffee machine. I owe her big time.

'It's nothing! A mere suggestion ...'

'... that could save my ass.'

'Bit dramatic, Alanis.'

*

I talked to Rob. There were several clauses in the fine print, a list of terms and conditions, and some serious sucking up on my part, but eventually Rob agreed to let me use the courtyard for Paigefest. I've spent the last hour calling all the bands and confirming – it's all happening next Friday. I think I've pretty much done all I have to and now it'll be up to the musicians to perform and the crowd to turn up. It's just meant to be a friends-of-friends thing but given that everyone seems to know everyone around here it could be huge. I remember that it's also my first time playing solo and feel a jolt of nervous energy.

I call Spike again. He still doesn't answer.

I leave another message. 'Hey, Spike. It's me. Hope you're okay. I miss you. Please call me. Also, I really hope you can come to the gig next Friday. Caz helped me get Vinyl as the venue. In the courtyard. I'll be making my solo debut! It would mean a lot to me if you were there. Also, my Alanis gig is also next weekend. Oh, it was Caz who signed me up for that, for the record. I'm sorry I've been so awful. No excuses. Just really sorry. And … uh, yeah, I miss you.' My voice cracks a bit at the end.

As soon as I hang up my phone rings again. I answer immediately. 'Spike?'

'Nope, it's me.'

'Oh, Rose. Rose! How are you?' It's been a shamefully long time.

'Okay, but I haven't heard from you in ages. Haven't you been getting my messages?'

'I'm sorry. I'm so busy and then I had this argument with Spike and I've been feeling so bad.' It all comes pouring out.

'Oh, little sister.'

'I was horrible. I'm such a selfish person.'

'You are not. I'm sure you're doing your best. Besides, selfish people don't beat themselves up for being selfish.' I love Rose. I should have called her ages ago.

'Your messages … were they about Mum stuff?' I know I read them, but I can't remember the content.

'Mum updates mostly. She's no worse than when we went to see her. I'm thinking of going again.'

I feel a jolt of panic that she might ask me to go with her. Selfish, see?

'I know it's hard for you to get here, so don't feel bad if you can't make it.'

'You're such a good person, Rose,' I blub.

'I try.'

'I should try harder.'

'Yes, you should.' She's teasing, but it's true.

'Screw you. But seriously ...' I hear myself rambling away about me again.

'Look, I'm sure you'll sort it out. Spike *looooooves* you – he'll forgive you, I'm sure.'

So, I tell her everything. It sounds silly and adolescent when I say it out loud and much less dire.

'Relationships, huh?' she says. 'Just ... I don't know. Slow down, listen to people. Try not to get all Paigey about stuff.'

'What's that supposed to mean?'

'You know, all defensive and offended when people point out your failings.'

It's all I can do not to get all 'Paigey' about that. I groan.

'You've got this,' she says. 'And stay in touch, little sister! I'm just a hit reply away.'

'I will, I will, I promise.' I catch myself. 'How are you anyway? What's been happening in your life?' I try to focus on Rose's reply, but my mind is all over the place.

twenty-two

People keep telling me to calm down and that's about the least helpful thing anyone could possibly say to me right now. It's really winding me up.

Rob's setting up the PA out in the courtyard, but it seems to be a sweary middle-aged tangle of leads and extension cords at this point. Caz is lighting the gas heaters and setting up an outdoor bar. Max is here with most of his drum kit and I'm pacing around wondering where the hell everyone else is. We need to start soundcheck.

'There's heaps of time, Paige. It's all okay,' Caz says from behind a stack of sound gear. 'Besides, these are rock musicians. They're not going to be expecting – or even wanting – things to happen without a glitch or two.'

'There will be no glitches!' I shout.

'Wow. Okay. Sorry.' Caz leaves me to it.

Taylor turns up, all charm and cheer and chatter. 'Paigefest is go!' He raises the guitar he's carrying in the air, as if he has just announced an official launch with his own presence.

I scowl at him.

'Woah. What's up, Paige? You look stressed out.'

'I am stressed out! Where have you been? And it's not Paigefest!' The flyers called it A Midwinter Jam at Vinyl so I'm going with that, even if it's not the most catchy title.

'Sorry, sorry. I know we're late, but there's heaps of time, right? We're all here now. What do you need?'

I look around the courtyard. Caz has set up the fairy lights and seating and outdoor heaters. It actually looks beautiful, and I start to chill a little.

Rob lets out a grunt and tugs on the end of another extension cord. I nod towards him and say quietly to Taylor, 'Maybe you could give Rob a hand with the rig?'

Taylor goes over and gives a kind of 'yikes' expression when he sees the tangle. He introduces himself to Rob who shakes his hand and happily accepts the assistance.

Nate's helping Max set up the drum kit and shuffling things into a stage shape, setting up microphones and amps. I see he's brought his favourite Fender Tweed amp for the occasion.

I check my phone and send a much-cheerier-than-I'm-feeling-right-now message to all of tonight's performers, telling them how excited I am. It's a gentle reminder that they're supposed to be here already for soundcheck.

A van pulls up bringing Virginia's Wolf. I help carry their gear through the café and out to the courtyard. A few punters have wandered in and I find myself heaving a double bass past a couple who evidently see no reason to get out of my way. Charlie wheels her keyboard through with a much more assertive, 'Scuse me, mate.' Maree joins Max at the kit on the stage. She's brought her congas and chimes and the percussion section starts looking pretty epic. Tess helps Nate adjust the mics.

I take a minute to watch my friends, colleagues and fellow musicians mingling. I wonder what alliances might be formed tonight and what amazing musical collaborations could evolve from this. I've done everyone a service, and this thought makes me smile. It's going to be okay.

When Lou and Lex turn up, the Spike-shaped gap I

was trying to ignore feels spot-lit. I'm relieved Lou's here though. I've hardly seen her recently.

'Yay, Lou! You're here. Wait. Where's your keyboard?' She's empty-handed.

'I was hoping to borrow one. There's one.' She points at Charlie who's setting up her stand and plugging in.

'Assuming you could borrow one, you mean. Why didn't you bring your Casio?' I already know the answer – it's not really stage-worthy. I just can't believe how entitled she can be. 'You'd better go ask Charlie. And be nice about it,' I say.

Lou raises her eyebrows and I'm worried she'll burst into tears.

'Sorry. I'm sure it's probably fine, but you do have to ask.'

'Yes, you do,' Lex backs me up.

Lou shrugs and nods. I smile so she doesn't have a tantrum. Lex goes with her and adds his cymbals to what's becoming the most impressive looking kit ever.

Other musicians trickle in, adding their gear to the stage. It's good to see Mel and Shaun and the Goldlust guys again.

If I wasn't trying to give Spike space, I would have asked him to do sound for this event. As it is, Rob has volunteered to be on the sound desk. He's not incompetent, but he is a bit grumpy. He starts bossing us around and soundcheck begins at last – Agent Smith first, then Rob asks me to do a little test for my solo set. I feel so exposed when the rest of the band leave the stage area. I take out the acoustic/electric guitar I borrowed from Greg and play through one song until the levels are okay. Then I quickly leave the stage. As the other bands check their sound and a few more arrive, I start to feel the weight of responsibility lift off my shoulders. It's going well. From here, the bands will look after themselves.

The evening grows dark and the space remains pretty empty. Maybe I should have scrapped the door charge, although that was one of Rob's conditions. I glimpse him twiddling knobs on the sound desk. It's one of the coldest nights we've had in weeks, a deeply bone-chilling cold that came on suddenly in the afternoon. People are congregating under the gas heaters. Have I wasted everyone's time?

Each act will perform for fifteen minutes and there will be two sets. Timing needs to be pretty exact so that everything's wrapped up by eleven (another Rob condition). Five minutes turnaround between acts and half an hour between sets.

Agent Smith starts right on eight. The place is still filling, but we're used to playing to all sorts of crowds. I keep an eye out for Spike. He's still not here. If he doesn't show, will it feel like the whole night was a disaster?

Taylor catches my eye and gives me a wink. Agent Smith sounds good and people are moving closer and nodding along. I force myself to zone back into the moment, feel the weight of my bass hanging from my shoulder, fingers on the strings. The music is larger than just my part, it's all of us – musicians and audience. I grin at Taylor, as he moves forward to add backup vocals to the chorus.

Nic Cage and the Bad Leads and then Ghostwriters keep the first set moving along. It's not until Ghostwriters announce their last song that I get hit by a wave of nerves. My solo set is up next, just before the break. I start actually shaking. How can I perform with this sudden loss of motor control?

'Are you all right?' Lou asks.

'Yeah. Just freaking out a bit about my solo,' I confess.

'You'll be fine. I used to get nervous, but it becomes second nature after a while.' I remember what Taylor once told me about nervousness being better than complacency.

How can I harness these shakes to my advantage?

'You don't get nervous anymore?' I ask Lou. 'You're first up for the second set.'

She smiles. 'I'll be fine,' she says and turns back to the band.

I roll my eyes.

Suddenly Ghostwriters have finished and everyone's cheering and clapping as they leave the stage.

Shit. I'm up.

I feel hot and clammy and my chest is throbbing, but I'm heading up there and unpacking my borrowed guitar. I fumble the lead as I plug in, fumble the strings as I tune. I twist my hair up into a topknot and as I step behind the microphone, the feeling instantly changes. This feels good. I lower the mic and say hi, trying not to notice people heading for the door. It's okay. I've got this.

'Hi, I'm Paige. Thanks so much for coming tonight! And thanks to the amazing performers we've seen so far.'

A squeal of feedback. I glare at Rob.

'I'm going to play some songs I've been writing, then we're going to take a short break before our second set. I hope you like them.'

I start with some of the ones I wrote after visiting Mum. They're a bit sorrowful, but that's kind of the point. I hope the audience will feel something as they listen.

Before I know it, I've come to my last song – the one I wrote after that argument with Spike. I wonder if he's here to hear it. I can't see him, but I decide to say something just in case.

'This is my last song. Thank you for making my solo debut so wonderful. This song is for someone I care about a lot. But I messed up and I miss him terribly. I hope he's listening.' And with that, I bear my soul to the huge, attentive crowd.

I walked home alone
another night when streets turn dark too fast
the trams don't stop, they just roll past
I should have stayed at home

When you and I were young
we walked home from school together
played records, changed the weather
you said, 'Here comes the sun.'

For years you weren't around
and there were gaps throughout my sound
I need a lead tune for my bassline
to lead you when we ride, there was a time
when you were my guitarist
but now I'm just
playing solo with my heart
sprawled on the bed
when you should be lying here beside me.

I went out alone
to a party filled with wide-eyed fools
they laughed at me and broke the rules
I should have stayed at home.

When you and I were young
we never talked about you leaving
you moved north and left me grieving
said, 'Wish you were here.'

In those years you weren't around
there were gaps throughout my sound
I need backup vocals in the chorus
you to back me when I'm raucous

you were my best friend
but in the end
I'm left playing solo with my heart
spread on my sleeve
when you should be up on stage beside me.

*

During the break, I go and thank the bands. A few have already left, but the others assure me they're enjoying the gig. The vibe sparks and glows like the courtyard. Rob plays some records, people order drinks. I get a few pats on the back for my solo and the tightness in my chest shifts a little.

I haven't seen Spike anywhere.

Lou starts getting ready. After her is Virginia's Wolf and Goldlust. This half is more of a mixed bag, but a good note to end on, I hope.

Where is Spike? Will someone tell him I played a song for him? I try to enjoy the compliments and the atmosphere, but I'm anxious as hell – again.

'You were great!' Caz appears in front of me, hands me a drink and hugs me. 'Your song for Spike,' she puts a hand on her heart. 'Oh, sweetheart.' She hugs me again. My scarf falls to the ground, and I can't tell if she's taking the piss.

'Too cheesy?' I ask.

'Just cheesy enough. Where is he? He should be throwing himself into your arms after that.'

I bend down to retrieve my scarf. 'I don't know.'

'Ah,' Caz's tone changes.

'What?'

'It's like a Pixies song,' she says, nodding towards something behind me.

I turn and there he is. Caz pats my shoulder and slips

away.

He's gorgeous, a dimply smile twinkling like the fairy lights. 'Paige ...' he starts.

'I'm so sorry, Spike,'

'I'm sorry too,' he says. 'That song ...'

'You were here? I wrote it for you.' I was about to say, 'I'm in love with you', but suddenly we're kissing, and I hear something that sounds like fireworks, but is maybe just Caz popping a bottle of champagne behind the bar or just Lou testing out the mic or just a speaker blowing or just the fairy lights exploding. Maybe the party's over and everyone's left and it's just us standing here alone in the courtyard.

It doesn't matter.

twenty-three

I wake in Spike's arms. His bed and body are warm, and I've just had the best sleep of my life.

I try to move, but he pulls me closer, so I lie here, smelling of him, and look around his room. It's so him. Crates of records, amps, posters from gigs I've never heard of. There's a bookshelf of biographies and some tatty looking novels I want to browse through. His room has a much more lived-in feeling than mine. It almost feels more familiar to me. Then I spot the record cover I made for him two long years ago, back when he left school – the lyrics to 'You're Gonna Make Me Lonesome When You Go' spiralling around a collage of memories. It's framed on the wall.

When Spike wakes, he smiles at me and rubs his eyes. 'That was the best sleep I've had in years,' he says, and I laugh.

'Me too. It's good to see you.' I kiss him for a long time, my hands in his hair and his arms wrapped around me.

'Did you mean what you said last night?' he asks.

I look him in the eye, 'Absolutely.' Then, 'What did I say?'

'Well, lots of things, but the one I wanted to double check about is tonight. You're sure you want me there with you?'

'Oh yes! God yes! That was inspired. If you'll accompany me on the Alanis song it will be a million times better than if I tried to do it on my own.'

'Brilliant. We should probably practise it.'

'We should. I need to help with the pack out and clean up at Vinyl this morning though, so after that?' I feel slightly hyper.

*

The Midwinter Jam at Vinyl had kind of fizzled with the second set. Virginia's Wolf was all over the place and Maree cut our set short when she saw people were walking out. Lou's voice sounded kind of thin without backup and I guess I expected more from her solo stuff. I felt a bit bad for her, but when she bounced off the stage smiling, I didn't say anything, just gave her a hug. The dwindling crowd seemed to enjoy Goldlust though. Spike and I had huddled under the heaters and fairy lights until it was well and truly time to call it.

At Vinyl today, a steady stream of performers are collecting their gear – the reversal of last night's packing in.

Rob has packed up most of the sound gear by the time I arrive, so I tidy up, empty bins, make sure people are retrieving the right cymbal stands and power cords. Caz is working out the front and she makes me a hot chocolate.

Maree comes to collect her kit and stops to have a word.

'Thanks for the chance to play, Paige. That was ... well, I'm sure you put a lot of effort into making it happen. Cheers.'

'No worries. I'm sorry our set didn't quite gel.'

'It was a reality check, to be honest. A reminder to listen to my musician's intuition. The band's going to be taking an indefinite break. It's been fun getting to know you, though.'

That's a slap in the face, but I'm not really surprised. I feel a bit guilty for my role in the realisation, but also relieved. I was never a folk musician at heart.

Taylor arrives – it's always a bit of an event. He calls across the front of house to me. 'Paige! You're a legend. Last night was amazing.' A few customers look amused at how that sounds and I feel embarrassed.

'You think? The crowd was pretty thin,' I say when he's come closer and I can speak in an inside voice.

'Ah, crowd shmowd. I had fun. Free for practice tomorrow?'

'Sure thing.'

He grabs his guitar and exits.

As I'm leaving with my own gear, Rob stops me. Uh-oh. This might be too much for my hangover to handle.

'Just a minute, Paige. I just wanted to say, last night was a great idea. I enjoyed getting back on the sound desk. We should do it again.'

'We should?'

'Sure. Just needs a bit more dedicated organisation and some more marketing.'

'Right ...' I'm totally not putting my hand up for that.

'Anyway, let's see if we can get you a few more shifts here. Train you up on the coffee machine. I've rostered you on for Monday. Early. Don't be late!'

I see the ghost of a smile on his face.

twenty-four

'Hi, Dad.' I've called him this time. I'm so grown up.
'Paige, sweetheart, so good to hear from you!'
His big face is all smiley eyes, but he looks greyer than I
remember.

'I have so much news – things have been happening! I
organised this amazing event – well, actually it was a bit of a
flop, and one of my bands, umm ... disbanded because of it.
Oh, and turns out Lou is kind of an average solo performer.
But my boss was happy. And then on Saturday night Spike
and I played at an Alanis Morissette tribute gig. It was
ridiculous! All these people dressed up in flannel shirts were
singing along.'

Dad's laughing, 'Alanis Morissette? I remember.
Something about spoons?'

'Ha! Yeah, the line from her ironically unironic song
called 'Ironic'.'

'Tell me about it,' Dad says.

So I do. The Alanis gig was great. I'm so glad I got
Spike to perform with me, and 'You Learn' was an excellent
choice. Spike played the more complicated parts on guitar,
and I played a kind of rhythm and bass part and sang. He
joined me in the chorus, and it felt like we were one of those
loved up couples who stare into each other's eyes and sing
about our deep understanding of each other to an audience

that doesn't get it. At the time it felt perfect.

'I'm so glad everything's going so well.' Dad's speaking slowly and almost shouting as if I'm very far away. 'How are you going for money? Are you working in addition to all of this?'

'I haven't lost my job yet,' I joke, lamely. 'And Rob said he's going to find me a few more shifts.'

Dad looks decidedly unconvinced.

'I do get paid for gigs, too, you know. Seriously, Dad, I'm okay. Don't worry.'

'It's my job to worry. It was one of the terms and conditions I agreed to when you were born.'

I roll my eyes.

*

I'm listening to *Blue* and tapping on my phone when Spike appears in my bedroom doorway.

'Is this Joni Mitchell?' He puts down his guitar case and lies next to me on my bed.

'Yeah, "My Old Man." One of my favourites.'

'What are you up to?' He asks.

'Group chat with Molly and Lily.' I put my phone away and turn the music down. 'They're going to go to the festival with us! Well, they said they'd try to.'

'Cool! We've got planning to do then,' Spike says.

'We do! Starting with convincing Lou that Lou Key and the Lunar Three must play a gig there! We need to tactfully tell her she's crap without us. That can be your job,' I joke.

'The Lunar Three need their fifteen minutes of fame! Even if that's the only gig we ever play.'

'I totally agree. Lou's in her room. Go tell her now.'

Spike laughs. 'Maybe later. What else will we need to organise? We'll need camping gear and transport ...'

'Let's make lists!' I grab my notebook and we sit together cross-legged on my bed.

I'm making plans with Spike. This is how it's going to be. Whether we wind up playing at or just attending the festival, without a car, we're going to have to rely on our band mates quite a bit. We start brainstorming the equipment we'll need to beg, borrow or purchase.

I look around my room. I only have a few more items than when I first moved in – a growing pile of records, my Victrola, a couple more books. The guitar I borrowed from Greg lies behind me on the bed and my bass sunbursts from where it's propped in a corner.

The cover of *Chronicles: Volume One* peeks out from under a pile of clothes on the floor. Absentmindedly I imagine my own biography: 'When Paige Bell moved to Melbourne on the twenty-fourth of January ...' Then my mind changes time signature.

'Hey! I've got an idea.' I leap up. I hand Spike his guitar and grab Greg's from the bed. 'Come with me.'

'Come ... where? Now?'

'Yes! Now!' I take his hand and lead him downstairs. 'We're going out.'

Spike and I carry our guitars through the warm spring day to a spot outside Barkly Square. I crouch down to open my case.

'What's happening?' he asks, but he knows exactly what's happening. He looks around at the Sunday crowd: a couple of older guys sitting on a bench, shoppers, dog walkers passing. A small kid is sitting on the ground eating frozen yoghurt and some older kids are staring down at their phones.

'We're busking.' I look at him with a grin.

'I thought so.' He's apprehensive, but I'm not negotiating.

I open my case and stand behind to tune up. This will be a fully acoustic, unplugged performance. 'Come on! I'll start with something easy.' C G Am – a bit of Dylan to get us going.

Spike shakes his head, but joins in, maybe to prevent me from embarrassing myself, maybe because playing along to Dylan is utterly irresistible.

We're pretty messy and I don't blame the passers-by for passing on by, but it's so much fun. We run through our living room repertoire: Dylan, Nirvana, our Alanis song. I try the opening chords of Joni's 'All I Want' but give up. That one's going to need more practice. We sing our way through Ryan Adams' 'To Be Young' – Spike loses it trying to do falsetto in the bridge and I get the lyrics all mixed up.

I feel tears coming on. What would my life be like without these great songs? It doesn't bear thinking about. Someone tosses some coins into my guitar case and I strum the chords a little stronger, a little louder, so the sound travels all the way down that once lonesome road.

playlist

'Someday' The Strokes, *Is This It*

'Don't Think Twice, It's All Right' Bob Dylan, *The Freewheelin' Bob Dylan*

'There Is A Light That Never Goes Out' The Smiths, *The Queen Is Dead*

'This Flight Tonight' Joni Mitchell, *Blue*

'Bridge Over Troubled Water' Simon and Garfunkel, *Bridge Over Troubled Water*

'The Boy In The Bubble' Paul Simon, *Graceland*

'All I Want' Joni Mitchell, *Blue*

'Here Comes Your Man' The Pixies, *Doolittle*

'You Learn' Alanis Morissette, *Jagged Little Pill*

'My Old Man' Joni Mitchell, *Blue*

'To Be Young (Is To Be Sad, Is To Be High)' Ryan Adams, *Heartbreaker*

acknowledgements

I acknowledge the Traditional Custodians of the land on which this book was written, the people of the Kulin Nation, and pay my respects to Elders past, present and future.

A huge thank you to Anna Golden, who assessed an early version of this novel and later revisited it with the enthusiasm and attention needed to bring it back to life. Thank you Kellie Book Design for the beautiful design and to Nic Scurry for the thorough and no-doubt tedious job of proofreading. Thank you to my grandparents, Kay and Noel Marsh, for helping me set up this little imprint and get this book to an audience.

Thank you to my mum, Jan Marsh, for the endless support and encouragement; to Mary McCallum for the advice; Richard Wise for the writing space; and to a host of Melbourne musicians for the backstage passes and insights into your world.

Thank you Jason and Lotus for everything.